D0834282

# DEATH
# ON THE
# HIGH C's

Robert Barnard

A DELL BOOK

Published by
Dell Publishing Co., Inc.
1 Dag Hammarskjold Plaza
New York, New York 10017

Dell ® TM 681510, Dell Publishing Co., Inc.

ISBN: 0-440-11900-6

Reprinted by arrangement with Walker Publishing Company, Inc.

Printed in the United States of America

One Previous Dell Edition

New Dell Edition

First printing—June 1985

# DEATH
## on the
# HIGH C'S

# CHAPTER I

## Some Vocal Exercises

The Pitford Independent Methodist Hall hadn't known singing like it in many a long day, not since the people of that sorry Manchester suburb had poured their hearts into fervent hymns that kept their minds off poverty, disease, and the temptation of gin. For years, in fact, it had not known singing of any kind at all, and it was on account of its semi-derelict condition that the Northern Opera Company had been able to hire it so cheaply.

'This is one place where you really might bring the house down,' Mike Turner had said to Gaylene Ffrench, as they rather glumly surveyed the rickety old Independent Methodist caretaker.

Economy was of the essence. The Northern Opera Company had been going for a year, shuffling between Manchester and Liverpool, and kept alive by a tiny grant from the Arts Council. The powers-that-be in the world of arts' financing naturally channelled their big grants to London, on the principle of 'to him that hath', and they told Mike Turner, director of the fledgling company, that the organization would have to 'prove itself artistically' before it could expect a larger share of

the national cake. The phrase had been much discussed in the company, and Owen Caulfield, who
had done most of the routine rehearsing during
the first year, said that the required proof would
be that the Prime Minister should choose to miss
the Durham Miners' Gala in order to attend a first
night. Others said it would be when Birgit Nilsson
expressed herself willing to sing Third Norn in the
Company's *Ring*. All were agreed that it would be
a long process.

The first new production of the season was to
open on 15 September. It was to be *Rigoletto*, and
Owen Caulfield was to be rewarded for the hard
labour of the past year with the first new production of his own. Without liking him very much, the
company as a whole was glad for him, and felt that
the management was nursing up its own talent.
Gaylene Ffrench, it is true, pointed out that in
view of the sum they were paying their guest
soprano the management had been forced to
economize on a producer, but that was a Gaylene
remark, and nobody took too much notice. The
Pitford Methodist Hall was to be used for the
early rehearsals, and the company meanwhile had
opened its season with more performances of their
successful *Bohème* of last year and a tragi-comic
*Lohengrin*, for which they had secured sets and
costumes from the long-defunct Carl Rosa Company. And Manchester was coming. Manchester
was sobbing at *Bohème*, and sniggering at *Lohengrin*, but Manchester was coming. 'I'm sure *that's*
not what they mean by proving ourselves artistically,' said Calvin Cross, as he took a curtain-call as
Rodolfo, and gazed into the dark cheering depths

of the Prince of Wales Theatre. And, sadly, he was
right.

It was Calvin Cross who, on a windy day in the
middle of August, sang the first real notes in the
Pitford Methodist Hall, other than a few chesty
hoots that Gaylene Ffrench had let fly experimentally on her visit with Mike Turner. Calvin had the
key, because he had lodgings only a few streets
away, and when, on that first day of rehearsal, he
let himself, Gaylene and Bridget Lander in, he surveyed the dim, cobwebbed interior which the local
chars had been able to make little impression on,
and with a strong sense of the inappropriate he expanded his lungs and sang to the most distant
rafter:

'Bella figlia dell'amo—o—ore.'

It was a sweet tenor voice, and the hall, which
in its time had made hollow, hungry voices sound
strong and full, did its best for Calvin's. It sounded
very seductive indeed. He turned with a delighted
grin to Bridget: 'Splendid little hall,' he said.

'Not so much of this Eyetalian,' said Gaylene
Ffrench, stomping over to the far end of the hall
and dumping down on a stray chair the bulging
plastic bag that contained her sustenance for the
day. 'We're doing the thing in English, guest star
notwithstanding.'

She undid the top button of her blouse, threw
apart her arms, and bellowed, 'Land of Ho—ope
and Gllory!' Then she put her hands on her hips,
looked at the pair by the door with infinite self-
satisfaction, and said: 'If the hall'll stand that, it'll
stand anything.'

Gaylene was a strong, stumpy Australian lass,

running rapidly to flesh, but with some brassy
good-looks that could go quite a long way in the
hands of a capable makeup artist. She had an
aggressive bust, and, off-stage, the stance of a suf-
fragette about to heave a brick through a Down-
ing Street window. She had dithered between
singing and competitive athletics at school, but
when she reached fifteen without making the big
time at hurdling or swimming she had opted for
the activity in which she would not flower and
fade so fast. She was now at full bloom. In ten
years' time she would probably have put on so
much weight that her Delilah would be ridiculous,
and even as Amneris she would need careful cos-
tuming.

At present it was her recent Carmen with the
Welsh National that was fresh in everyone's mind.
Brazen, blatant, torrid and vulgar, it had had some
critics reaching for their superlatives, and others
simply reaching. She even claimed that one Non-
conformist minister had preached a sermon against
her somewhere in the valleys, but nobody believed
her. It was as well not to believe Gaylene when she
said things of this sort. In fact, it was rumoured
that when she said she had sung at the opening of
the Sydney Opera House, this should be translated
as meaning that she had been in the audience and
had joined in the National Anthem. People reacted
in different ways to Gaylene, most of them hostile,
and her career since she came to England eighteen
months before had not been unmarked by theatrical rows and upsets: she had once had her face
clawed by the soprano soloist in *Messiah*, as they
trooped off the platform, in full view of sections of

the reverently applauding audience. Bridget Lander said she could stand Gaylene in small doses, but as Calvin remarked, small doses was exactly what one never got Gaylene in.

'I suppose we'll be doing the third act today, will we?' asked Bridget.

'Natch,' said Gaylene. 'Most important act.' It was the only one she was in. 'Owen told me in bed last night. Said we'd use nearly half the rehearsal time on that act—the others are more or less plain sailing, according to him.'

'So much for my best scenes,' said Bridget ruefully.

'Well, so what?' said Gaylene, putting her hands on her hips as she did when she wanted to let fly with an unpalatable truth, or untruth: 'You're only a stand-in. You'll be out on your little pink ear as soon as Signora Spaghettini arrives.'

'Giulia Contini,' said Calvin. 'And Bridget will be singing in the January performances.'

'That's as maybe. Don't know that I'll be in it myself by then. I had an offer from Germany today—they're wild to get me in *Carmen.*'

'Oh?' said Calvin, scenting a lie. 'Which company?'

There was a pause which confirmed his guess.

'Bonn,' said Gaylene finally. It was the town she had heard of most frequently in news summaries.

'*Not* one of the major companies,' said Calvin. 'Hardly worth learning the translation for.'

The others started drifting in then. Owen Caulfield came, as usual, at full pace, with plenty of noise and bustle. Everything Owen did was a little too loud, a little too fast. Beneath a surface ami-

ability there was a constant need to make his
presence felt, his superiority acknowledged. The
translation from blandishment to hectoring was
too ready, and everyone waited for it, tense. He
was medium-sized, lean, edgy, and greying before
his years, and people wondered whether he would
burn himself out before he really got anywhere.
Though today was only a vocal run-through which
he was supposed merely to be sitting in on, he was
impelled to organize everyone into his own sort of
efficiency: little Mr. Pettifer, the repetiteur, was
seated at the piano and told when he could start,
the cast was bustled into positions around him, and
when Owen sat down to listen everyone could feel
him itching to produce them. Damn him, they
thought: this is a vocal rehearsal.

The early rehearsals were to be in Italian. Mike
Turner, the company's director, who was to con-
duct, was insistent on this. If they knew the Italian,
this would smooth over the early rehearsals with
Giulia Contini when she arrived, and in any case
a thorough knowledge of the text helped singers to
project the words of the translation. They would
change to the English version when la Contini had
been to a few rehearsals. So when Simon Mulley,
the veteran Rigoletto, began the apparently com-
monplace dialogue with Gilda that begins Act III,
he said: '*E l'amo?*' and Bridget replied: '*Sempre.*'
It is a simple word, set simply, but there was an
immediate stillness. Even Owen seemed for a moment to stop planning moves and gestures and
novel approaches and really to listen.

No one in the company except Mike Turner had
heard Bridget before. She had had a great success

in a little-known Donizetti opera while still a student at the Guildhall School. It was on the strength of this and a few performances with semi-amateur groups that she had been engaged. She was to sing the tiny role of the Countess Ceprano, and to stand in as Gilda for the distinguished guest soprano until she arrived. Later, as Calvin had said, she would get her chance in the star role. What she would make of it could only be guessed, but even as she and Simon sang that huddled, almost surreptitious dialogue the voice was revealed as clean, pure, and wonderfully controlled. Calvin gave her a look of encouragement and admiration. Gaylene Ffrench gave her a look of quite another kind.

The introductory dialogue began losing its muffled character as the Duke and Sparafucile entered, and Mr. Pettifer modulated into a surprisingly sprightly account of the accompaniment to 'La donna è mobile'.

The action at this point of *Rigoletto* is one thing about opera that everybody knows. The Duke, lured to a lonely tavern kept by the murderous thug Sparafucile and his sister Maddalena, is watched by Gilda, the girl he has seduced, and Rigoletto, the father who has sworn vengeance. He sings with a libertine cynicism of the fickleness of women, and the music reflects the speciousness and superficiality of his argument and his life: it is lilting, carefree, insincere. Calvin's first shot was like most first shots: it was a nice enough sound, but a little heavy. When he finished with a passable flourish, Calvin made a scowl of dissatisfaction with his effort. As usual at moments when no underlining was needed, Owen felt he had to make things explicit: 'You're supposed to be a libertine Duke,' he said in that high tone which was meant to be bantering, 'not a Conservative politician.'

'OK, I know,' said Calvin. 'It's tough trying to sparkle so soon after breakfast. It'll come, it'll come.'

'Take it again,' said Owen.

Calvin allowed a moment's pause.

'Would you like me to try it again?' he said to Mr Pettifer, trying to convey his opinion of who ought to be in charge of this rehearsal. Mr Pettifer just smiled vaguely, and immediately began the accompaniment. A trace of roughness entered Calvin's second account of the area. When he finished, Owen sat hunched in his seat, his hand meditatively on his jaw, very obviously saying nothing.

With the entry of Maddalena, the tavern whore, a new urgency enters the music. Maddalena has only a short time in this one act to make an effect, and Gaylene was a singer who would make sure she achieved an effect of one sort or another. The music was racy and seductive, and Gaylene, hands on hips, delivered it with a bouncy vulgarity, too loud. There was something else wrong too, for the voice didn't quite suit the part: there was a suggestion of British Contralto about it, a touch of the Kathleen Ferriers. The listener felt that she might be better employed telling good tidings to Zion, though Gaylene did not in any other respect suggest a messenger of the Lord, and would not for a moment have accepted her unsuitability for the role of Maddalena if anyone had had the temerity to suggest it. It was a role in which the singer could give full rein to any blowsiness and vulgarity at her command, and Gaylene intended to give it plenty. Vocally she regarded it as her job, in this and any other role, to outsing the rest: Gaylene opened her mouth, and apparently without any physical effort she sang twice as loud as anyone else.

'Gaylene, darling,' said Calvin as they finished the ensemble, 'you are bellowing.'

'I am not bellowing!' bellowed Gaylene. 'Just try giving it a bit more go yourself.'

'Either I am an elegant aristocrat, or I'm a coal-heaver,' said Calvin. 'We'd better make up our minds right from the start. And Verdi thought he was an aristocrat.'

'Well, I'm a whore,' said Gaylene. 'And whores are loud.'

'Physically, dear girl,' said Simon Mulley, in his quiet, polite way. 'Not vocally.'

'Cut the character analysis, will you?' said Owen. 'That's my business. Try it over again, and give it a bit more power, Calvin, and you try muffling it a bit, Gay.'

They went through it again, Calvin effortlessly giving it a modicum more volume, his self-esteem tempting him to show that he could, and Gaylene giving full rein to her trumpet tones as before, only on the isolated phrase hushing it to a whisper, with a satirical glance at Calvin.

Mr Pettifer, the repetiteur, thought it tactful to go straight on into the quartet.

'*Bella figlia dell'amore*,' sang Calvin, for the second time that morning, as sweetly and seductively as if he had imbibed honey and molasses with his mother's milk. '*Schiavo son de' vezzi tuoi*.' The tone caressed the air, full of sex and mischief, full of delight and faithlessness. Perhaps it was inadvertence that made Calvin, in the course of these opening lines, turn toward Bridget. Whatever it was, the beauty of his singing didn't prevent Gaylene hissing at him in a stentorian whisper: 'It's me you're supposed to be bedding at this point, and don't you forget it.'

Without batting an eyelid, or turning a fraction in her direction, Calvin continued to the end, and Gaylene was too preoccupied with her own part to make further objections. After her skittish phrases, the pseudo-hesitations of the part-time whore—done in a somewhat flat-footed manner on this occasion—Simon Mulley, as Rigoletto, and Bridget, as Gilda, entered the fray. Now the rest could get a real idea of the quality of Bridget's voice, as it floated with effortless power over the others', framing their utterance and seeming to comment on them, by its purity and beauty. The silvery sound, swelling and diminishing, soared to heaven at the climaxes with the sort of poignancy that makes audiences stop their breath and wish that time could be suspended.

In spite of their preoccupation with their own singing, it gradually got through to everyone in the hall that what they were hearing was not a Mimivoice. Mimi-voices are very nice, but while they are not exactly two a penny, Britain does rather breed them, as she breeds collies and football hooligans. This was something more. Now Bridget was singing Gilda, soon it would be Violetta, perhaps Leonora. Eventually—who could say? Every heart in the hall was suddenly gripped by the conviction that they were witnessing the small beginnings of a rather splendid career. Not every heart was affected by this thought in the same way, but most of them missed a beat as they thought of the splendours and dangers of such a career, and the ease with which such a voice could be driven to ruin. As the voices threaded the argument to its silly conclusion the singers around Bridget swung towards her and started applauding, Calvin grinning wildly, Simon Mulley, as usual, making something elaborate and formal of it. Raymond Ricci, who as Sparafucile had no part in the quartet and had been lounging over by the old pulpit, looking long, black and saturnine in polo-neck sweater and tight cotton slacks, actually jumped into the air and clapped his hands over his head. And Mr Pettifer, who might have been expected to have grown cynical in a lifetime spent in coaching mediocre voices towards adequacy, beamed with pleasure and banged the lid of his piano in appreciation.

It was the sort of demonstration that any rival singer with an ounce of intelligence would have made sure that she took a part in. Generosity is a very easy emotion to counterfeit. But Gaylene Ffrench was a child of nature. Emotions flitted over her face like captions in the silent cinema, and she could no more hide her irritations, her jealousies, her contempts, than a dog could hide its interest in a bone. On this occasion she looked in the direction of the little demonstration with ill-concealed scorn, and said: 'Oh, for Christ's sake. This is a rehearsal, not a mutual admiration society.'

Nobody took any notice, and the fact that nobody was in a hurry to get back to rehearsing gave Owen Caulfield, stirring uneasily in his chair by the wall, the chance to butt in with: 'OK. Enough's enough. Shall we get on now, then?'

Somehow Owen often managed to touch a nerve in a way that Gaylene, with all her loud obviousness, never did. Simon Mulley turned on him.

'This is a vocal rehearsal. As singers we are paying tribute to a fellow artist. The emotion which prompts this is not one that you would recognize or understand.'

There was a complete silence. Such a defiance would normally be the occasion for one of Owen's outbursts, a bout of shouting tinged with hysteria, followed by a little mock-penitence and a great show of making it up with everybody. But Simon was not an ordinary member of the company. The integrity of his artistic standards and the misfortunes of his career gave him a position of unique respect in any company. His life in opera had been marked by brief moments of brilliant success, followed by resignations, rows, withdrawals. To compromise, to accept the shabby, the routine, the second-best which is part of life in an opera-house, was difficult for Simon. To do something with less than full seriousness, to give any work he was in anything but entire love and respect was impossible. He was now forty-five, a great artist who had never had a great career. He would stay in Manchester as long as he was convinced of the seriousness of the company. If he began to doubt that, he would go. This everyone knew. So after his outburst, which had a touch of the theatrical which in Simon was not insincerity, but part of his character, Owen Caulfield was silent. He sat down, and once again buried his chin ostentatiously in his hand.

After that, the rehearsal went smoothly enough. Gilda was killed, vocally, and put in her sack; Calvin managed the reprise of 'La donna' with much more panache, but Bridget seemed a little damped by the battle of words earlier, and the final duet did not quite have the pathos and beauty all had been expecting. But when they broke up they were most of them moderately pleased with themselves. Calvin and Bridget stood talking by the door and looking out into the tentative sunshine, he leaning elegantly against the doorpost, and both entirely taken up with themselves, each other, and their music. Simon Mulley dragged a seat over by Mr Pettifer, and they both went concentratedly over the moment of Rigoletto's opening of the sack, wrestling with the music and its emotional implications. Raymond Ricci and Gaylene went into a close huddle in the corner where she had dumped her bags, but they were not discussing music.

Owen was alone and unnoticed. It was moments like this that he feared, that set up inside him a panic sense that he had no existence, that presented him with a vision which he knew was not true, but which terrified him—the vision that he was nothing more than a noisy space. He stood irresolute in the centre of the Hall, half trying to look as if he were thinking and planning, half hoping that someone would call him in on their discussions. They were all being so damned *musical*, he thought—as if you could divorce it from the rest, from all those other parts of the pie in which he could legitimately plant his finger. Wanting to belong, incapable of belonging, Owen stood immobile for some minutes in the centre of the Hall. Then, as if at a signal, all the groups began to break up and drift out. As they came out into the watery sun and the crunching grime of the streets, Calvin and Bridget, too absorbed to think of bidding farewells, drifted off in the direction of a Wimpy Bar.

Owen turned to Gaylene. 'Lunch as usual?' he said.

'Jeez, you're slow,' said Gaylene. 'I take first comers, you know that.'

And she put her arm around Raymond Ricci's waist, and he—slim, lithe, sallow, and strangely Mephistophelean in his tight black garb—draped his arm around her shoulder, and they walked off down the shabby little street. Their bodies, intertwined yet ill-assorted, somehow seemed to work together, to form some sort of instant intimacy.

Owen watched them go, and turned abruptly in the direction of his car. His face was quite blank.

# CHAPTER II

*Mezzo Forte*

It was not until several days later, when things were well under way, and the shape of the production was already becoming clear, that Calvin and Bridget really got down to a concentrated discussion of their parts, and the way things in general were going. Bridget was in the kitchen of her ramshackle, roomy flat in Salford, cooking supper, and Calvin was stretched full length on the ancient sofa, relaxing after another successful performance of *Bohème*.

'The trouble with Owen,' shouted Calvin, over the sizzling hamburgers (both he and Bridget had healthy, undiscriminating singer's appetites), 'is that he's the typical dictator producer, but he doesn't have any interesting ideas to impose. So it all amounts to much ado about nothing. All that energy, all that shouting, all that finicky concern with detail—and what is it going to come out like in the end? The same old *Rigoletto* everyone's seen a thousand times.'

'He hasn't a great deal of imagination,' agreed Bridget, appearing at the kitchen door. 'He's got all the detail worked out, every gesture, and he's had one or two good ideas about the set. But it doesn't add up to much yet.'

'All this fiddling,' said Calvin, 'all this regimentation, and in the end you're back with the old Carl Rosa or something—the same old rep production.'

'Of course, in the long run that may be all to the good,' said Bridget, to be fair. 'It's a production that's got to last, and there's bound to be changes of singers the whole time—as we all get our summonses to Covent Garden or the Met.'

'I thought of La Scala for myself,' said Calvin agreeably. 'Oh yes, I agree—it's bound to be a bit workaday, but it doesn't have to be so *damned* standard. I think if we went about it the right way we could do something about it.'

'What, for example?'

'Well, humanize these puppets. You know, just a few small touches could make all the difference.'

Later, tucking in hungrily to their hamburgers, and periodically wiping the tomato sauce from around their mouths with the backs of their hands, they took the thing further.

'I don't go for the usual "cynical libertine" kind of interpretation of the Duke,' Calvin said. 'There is that element, but you've got to remember, his aristocratic background: he's always had any woman he wanted, and he's come to take that as a matter of course. I think he's sincere, passionate even, in his love for Gilda—as far as it's in his nature to be. When he's had her, he goes on to someone else—as he always has done. He loves the girl, but he's shallow, and naturally can't transcend his background.'

'If we were to do it like that,' said Bridget, 'then

Gilda wouldn't need to be the usual bird-brained slip who falls for the first handsome face she sees. I could try to fill her out a bit, give her a bit of initiative.' She grinned as she said: 'We could even try to show it as a clash between class behaviour patterns.'

'Not in Owen's production we couldn't,' said Calvin. 'You will be the silent-film heroine, and I will be the silent-film handsome seducer, if he has his way. But if we're careful, if we just slip in a few touches, without making an issue of them with Owen, we should at least be able to make a start at humanizing them. It would be interesting to try, anyway.'

They munched away strenuously for some minutes ('feeding my voice' Bridget called this to herself), and then she said: 'One thing we can be sure of: whatever we do, Gaylene's interpretation of Maddalena will remain . . . what shall we call it? Traditional?'

'Christ, what a bag,' said Calvin. 'I wish Bonn would offer for her Carmen. I'd whip round and raise the fare for her in a couple of shakes of her bosom.'

'I must say,' said Bridget, 'I thought when she came she was nervous and putting her worst foot forward. I now realize she was on her best behaviour.'

'You're lucky you don't have to act with her,' said Calvin. 'You don't have her clutching you to her bosom every other moment, whether called for or uncalled for, and brushing you sexily every time she passes you.'

'I don't think she'd bother to do that to me, even if I were acting with her,' said Bridget.

'You do wonder,' said Calvin, 'how she gets so many into bed with her. First Mike, then Owen, now Raymond. What do they see in her?'

'That should be obvious to the shortest sight,' said Bridget. 'But you notice she doesn't seem to keep them long.'

'She doesn't *want* them long,' said Calvin. 'She's voracious for variety. It's terrifying. It seems like she'll be satisfied with nothing less than saturation coverage.'

Bridget roared with laughter, wiped the crumbs from around her mouth, and they went on to other things.

A conversation of a quite different kind occurred that same evening in Gaylene Ffrench's apartment. She was leaning her massive contralto's shoulders against the bedstead and a wall of pillows and tucking appreciatively into an enormous slice of cream cake. Her splendid breasts, flopping randomly around the rapidly emptying plate, were being watched with slightly sardonic fascination by Raymond Ricci, who had stretched his naked saturnine length in the opposite direction, and was leaning his oily mediterranean head against the foot of the bed. He was smoking a long cigarette, and his eyelids were half-closed, giving his ordnance-survey consideration of Gaylene a cynical, amused, detached quality. Nobody, looking at them, would think that Raymond was very deeply involved. Come to that, nobody looking at Gaylene's rapt concentration on her cake would think she was either. When she had finished it, she drew her finger methodically over the plate, and sucked it. Then she said: 'That was good.'

'Thank you,' said Raymond Ricci.

'Not that,' said Gaylene. 'Big head.'

'You hadn't spoken since,' said Raymond. 'So I thought you might be paying an unexpectedly generous tribute to a fellow-artist.'

'If that's a crack about that Bridget girl,' said Gaylene, 'you can pipe down. I don't know what's gotten into you lot: you're all going out of your tiny pink minds about that young lady. Do her no good in the long run, you realize that, don't you? Voices like that are two a penny in Australia.'

'No, darling,' drawled Ricci, 'not even in God's own sun-baked, surf-riding, tennis-playing land are voices like that two a penny.'

'They are too,' said Gaylene, her voice beginning to bray, as it did when anyone was foolhardy enough to contradict her. 'What do you know about it, you pommie-wop? What counts is what you *do* with the voice, and if she's not careful she's going to take on all the big parts much too early, and end up as a singing teacher in Wup Wup. Mark my words.'

'Perhaps you should warn her,' suggested Raymond, his heavy-lidded eyes watching to see if his humour got through. 'That's the sort of thing that needs to be done tactfully—you know, the sisterly approach. You'd do it very well.'

His irony was lost on Gaylene.

'Stuff that,' she said briefly. 'Let her fry. I don't owe that young miss any good turns that I know of.'

Raymond stretched out his sallow length languorously, and scratched her ear with his big toe.

'It's you I'm thinking of, darling. You need to exercise a bit of discretion, or let's say wholesome deceit, anyway. We all know what this business is like: it's full of people elbowing their way to the top. The sensible ones put padding on their elbows. It softens the impact. With you, darling, one feels the hard bone in one's ribs.'

Gaylene looked at him for some moments, as if quite unsure of what he was trying to say. Then she screwed up her face, squared her obstinate shoulders, and said: 'If a thing needs saying, I say it. Straight out. It's the best way in the long run. And if you want to know the truth, I don't go much for your super-subtle, snake-in-the-grass pommie-wop ways, so put that in your pipe.'

This was the second time in the space of a few minutes that Gaylene had called Ricci a pommie-wop. Once she had got hold of a good line of attack or abuse, she rarely let it fall into disuse. Ricci was not greatly perturbed by racial sneers. He had a cat-like self-satisfaction, an utter assurance that he would come well out of any imaginable situation he might let himself get into, that made him quite unaffected by other peoples' opinions of him or his methods. Still, the crudity of it irritated him. He was fond of his parents, who had brought him to Britain when he was very young, in the early fifties, had worked hard to build up an Italian delicatessen in the unpromising suburb of Birmingham where he had grown up, and who had surrounded his childhood with adoration and music. In so far as he acknowledged any loyalties, it was to them.

And they returned it a thousand fold. He had a younger brother, a promising baritone, in the chorus of the Northern Opera, and his parents would travel miles to see any performance in which either of them was to appear. And when he thought about it, it seemed pretty ironic that Gaylene, who spent much of her professional life singing in the works of Italian composers, should regard his ancestry as a matter for crude racial abuse. But then Gaylene never thought, and therefore could never connect. She merely reacted. He wondered how long he would be able to put up with her brazen egotism, how long it would be outweighed by the sexual pleasures of her company. Not long, he thought. Not very long.

'Well, well,' he said, putting his head back on the mattress and letting his eyes rest on the dirty ceiling. 'Do it your own sweet way. Batter your way forward, bruise the shins of everyone in sight, tread on everybody's toes.'

'I intend to, if necessary,' said Gaylene.

'But don't be surprised if you get knocks and bruises yourself in the process. This is a nasty profession and there's no quarter given or asked: people climb over others, and then kick their faces down afterwards. Even the nicest of them know how to defend themselves.'

'Do you think I don't?' said Gaylene. 'I can give as good as any of this little lot.'

'Just don't come to me for help, that's all,' said Raymond.

'You know perfectly well what I come to you for,' said Gaylene. 'And it's about time you provided some of it.'

\* \* \*

That Thursday, in the second week of rehearsals,
the session at the Pitford Methodist Hall was to
start with the baritone-soprano sections from the
first act, and then was to go on to the inevitable
third act, which to Gaylene's gratification was
being given all the prominence which she had
prophesied—whether because it was (until the
chorus scenes came to be prepared) the most com-
plex scene, or whether because Owen wanted to
win his way back to Gaylene's bed, nobody knew.
Owen was not the sort of person whom one asked
to give reasons for his decisions.

Vocally the Act 1 scenes went very well. Bridget
and Simon were alone in the Methodist Hall, with
only Owen and Mr Pettifer. The lack of distraction
was beneficial: the working-out of all the problems
of balance and emphasis in the duets went like a
dream. Before that Simon's *Pari siamo* had been
intensely dramatic: Simon's strength was drama,
nuance, the stripping of hidden meanings. If he
had a fault, it was that the line of the music tended
to suffer. Here the line was less important than the
vigour of declamation:

*'Pari siamo! ...*
*l'uomo son io che ride, ei quel che spegne!'*

he sang. 'We are equals ... I am the man of laughter, and he of murder.' There was a shiver of self-
knowledge in the voice.

For the duets Bridget, after consulting with
Simon and Mr Pettifer, was determined not to stint
of voice. This Gilda was to be an emotional adult,

a woman who knew her own mind. Simon followed suit, opening up with the splendid, full line that was his when he didn't let his approach get too complicated by introspection.

Dramatically things did not go quite so well.

The stairs up to the pulpit represented the inevitable stairs up to Gilda's bedroom (why Gildas should almost invariably have those obliging stairs up to their bedroom is unclear, but Owen had accepted the tradition that this should be so). When Gilda came down them to meet her father, rushing impulsively, Owen objected: 'Too modern, Bridget. Come down *delicately.*'

'You mean *trip*, I suppose,' said Bridget.

'If you like, yes.'

'I'm not a *tripping* kind of person,' said Bridget.

'You are supposed, you know, to be playing a part,' said Owen reasonably enough but with that edgy, talking-to-idiots voice which did so much harm to the atmosphere at rehearsals.

Bridget tripped.

Later, as the duet worked up to its apprehensive, emotional climax, Bridget and Owen crossed swords again.

'Clasp your hands,' said Owen, entwining his fingers in a gesture of girlish supplication.

'Has anyone, ever, off the operatic stage, clasped their hands like that?' asked Bridget waspishly.

'Will you do just what I tell you to,' said Owen, his voice rising, 'and cut out the continual sniping?'

Bridget clasped her hands.

So there was already something of an atmosphere in the Hall by the time Gaylene and Ricci arrived separately for the rehearsal of the last act. Calvin was going through parts of *Bohème* with a new soprano at the theatre, and would be late. Gaylene bounced in, looking more than ever like a collapsed air-hostess, and flopped straight over to Owen.

'You poor fish,' she said. 'You look pooped. Have you been doing those ghastly long duets?' She lowered her voice to a tone of elphantine confidentiality. 'I don't know why you bother with those scenes. You'll have to go over them all again as soon as Signor Spaghettini arrives. Waste of good rehearsal time.'

She put her arm round the back of his chair, and Owen, seemingly rather grateful for her attention, entered into the intimate spirit of the scene.

'I've got to get the whole thing in my mind's eye,' he said. 'Put everything into place. The Italian will have to fit herself into my scheme of things. But you needn't worry: the last act will get its fair share of rehearsal time.'

'Oh Jeez, I'm not worried about that. I know what sort of performance I'm going to give, and rehearsals aren't going to change that very much. Give me a good sexy part like this, and I'm in it body and soul. But the others—well—' Gaylene gave a gigantic sniff—'they're a bit *English*, wouldn't you say? Stiff and reserved, like. If you ask me the lot of them need a firework up their backsides.'

'We haven't got all your wonderful Australian spontaneity,' said Raymond Ricci, lazily strolling over. 'Take Simon, for example: you may not believe this, but just occasionally he actually likes to

*think* about his part. You must find that curious—
but as a matter of fact, now and again I do too.'

'You'll never make a *real* opera-singer,' said Gaylene, unperturbed. 'You'll never *give a performance.* And nor will that wet prick Calvin, come to
that. Christ—the way I have to *work* on that weed.
And to date I've got precisely nowhere.'

'Perhaps,' said Bridget acidly, 'if you worked
less, you might get further. In any case, it's his
part that's important. You've got to let him work it
up in the way he wants it, and fit yourself into his
interpretation.'

'Stuff that,' said Gaylene contemptuously. 'He'd
do better to leave the ideas to Owen, and try working up a bit of passion instead. At the moment I'm
throwing myself at him the whole time, and the
most I get is a chaste hand placed lightly round my
waist. Talk about Victorian!'

'Passion isn't just a matter of two people throwing themselves around on top of each other,' said
Simon.

'Isn't it?' said Gaylene, for a moment looking
genuinely puzzled. Then her face cleared. 'But
you're too old. Probably hardly remember what it
was like.'

'You make it all much too obvious,' said Bridget
earnestly. 'And you nag him too much. You get his
back up.'

'Not at all the part of him she *wants* to get up,'
said Raymond softly.

Gaylene withdrew her arm from Owen's back,
and put out her tongue in Ricci's direction.

'I can get as much of that as I want any day of
the week, as you very well know. There's queues

from here to Manchester Central Station, as a matter of fact. In any case, in a week or so I'll be doing without the lot of you for a bit.'

'Some private form of Lent?' enquired Ricci politely.

'Shit you. My boy-friend's coming.'

'Boy-friend?' said Bridget. 'I didn't know you had a boy-friend.'

'Whadderyou mean?' brayed Gaylene. 'Why shouldn't I have a boy-friend? He's my fiancé actually, if you must know. And he could knock any of this collection of imitations of masculinity into the middle of next week, I'll tell you that.'

'Christ, Muhammed Ali,' said Ricci. 'I might have known no one else would take her on.'

'His name's Hurtle, if you must know,' said Gaylene. 'He's with the touring NSW Rugby team. they're coming to Manchester next week. He'll be staying a week or so.'

'Well,' said Bridget, 'that's nice. Perhaps we shall be able to rehearse some of the other bits of the opera that week.'

'Actually,' said Gaylene, 'by that time Signora Spaghettini will arrive, and you'll be back to two lines in Act I. Matter of fact, I'm looking forward to her coming. I'm hoping a bit of Latin passion might do the trick with poor old Calvin. Nothing else seems to raise a spark.'

'Gaylene,' said Bridget slowly, and with weighted emphasis, 'I'm getting a bit fed up with this continual sniping at Calvin. You'd better know, we got engaged last night.'

'What?' roared Gaylene, so shocked that she

stood up, her face twisted to a rare expression of outrage. 'What?'

'Engaged,' said Bridget. 'To be married.'

'But you can't,' said Gaylene. 'You just bloody can't.'

'Are you the only one allowed to have a fiancé?' asked Bridget.

'You can't marry *him*,' Gaylene shouted, red and furious. 'He's a nigger. He's a bloody black.'

She looked round at the others, and they in their turn could only look miserable and embarrassed. For what Gaylene said was quite undeniable. Especially as even now Calvin was standing in the doorway looking very black indeed.

# CHAPTER III

*Molto Agitato*

The publicity manager of the Northern Opera got a good deal of mileage out of the engagement of Bridget and Calvin. Even the *Guardian* put on its multi-racial hat and had a photograph of them. Calvin was the main point of interest, since he was already singing successfully with the company, whereas Bridget had only sung down South, and so could only be described as 'promising'. Then again, Calvin was black, and born British, and spoke the most impeccable English, and this (for some reason) thrilled most of the reporters to the depths of their liberal/radical souls. One of the reporters who had done some homework asked him if it was his ambition to sing Otello. 'If my voice grows by about three hundred per cent,' said Calvin. Another asked if he had found any examples of racial prejudice in the world of opera. To this Calvin cautiously replied that he found the audiences remarkably liberal-minded. The questioner seemed content with this.

It wasn't that Calvin was feeling particularly bruised by Gaylene's nasty little outburst, any more than Raymond Ricci had resented her 'pommie-wop' slurs. On the other hand, during Calvin's

life-time his race—and others of a similar black,
brown or dirty yellow shade—had taken over the
whole burden of British racial prejudice, which
had previously been distributed around, embracing
Italians, Irish, Germans, and Jews. The old preju-
dices had not really died: they had been subsumed
and concentrated into the more actual and immediate object. So though Calvin had been born in
Britain, to a family that had already been comfort-
ably settled in the country for two or three years,
he had had in his time his share of mindless insults,
of wanton rudeness or neglect in shops and restau-
rants, and more than his share of remarks prefaced
by 'Of course, there's nothing personal in this, but
in my opinion . . .'

Luckily the worst effects of hostility and ignorance had been cushioned by a stable home: his
parents were West Indian, his father had a good
job, comparatively, and they were churchgoers
who had integrated themselves into the community
years before 'integration' had become a problem
to be mulled over by politicians, leaders of opinion, and the heavy Sundays. Calvin had always
done well at school, and the chance at eleven to
play the Negro page in *Rosenkavalier* at Covent
Garden had sealed his fate. When his headmaster
had told him, a couple of years later, that he ought
to be thinking about Oxbridge, Calvin had said:
'I'm going to be an opera singer.' The headmaster
had pointed out, with a gentle smile, that as his
voice had not yet broken it was a little early to
decide that. 'Even if I sing like a cow with tooth-
ache, I'm going to be an opera singer,' Calvin had

said. Luckily the Good Lord had been in one of his rare obliging moods: Calvin got a voice.

So, after an initial reaction to Gaylene's remarks which was perhaps as much due to his general attitude to Gaylene as to racial feeling, Calvin calmed down, and laughed about it with Bridget in private. Still, he wasn't going to pretend to the gentlemen of the press that as far as the company was concerned everything in the racial garden was lovely, so he confined his remarks to the audiences, and everything was smoothed over.

On Monday morning, several members of the cast were relaxing in the Pitford Methodist Hall, in an interval between getting Act I, scene II into shape and starting in again on the unavoidable Act III. Inevitably, since like all singers and actors they loved publicity and had an implicit belief in its power, the papers were handed round, and a good deal of gentle ribbing of Calvin and Bridget took place.

'Obviously,' said Owen, who always tried to relax and be nice to his singers in the intervals of rehearsing, 'you're both being groomed as the new Jeanette MacDonald and Nelson Eddy.'

'Or perhaps Ted and Barbara Andrews,' said little Mr Pettifer, revealing an unsuspected vein of slyness. 'Their place has never really been filled.'

'No, thank goodness,' said Simon. 'I hope the management are suitably grateful for all the publicity you're bringing. They ought to throw a party for you both. I think I'll go to Mike and suggest it.'

'With the current financial situation of the company, I should think it would have to be a bring-

your-own-wine-and-cheese-party,' said Raymond
Ricci.

'We could all get together and arrange one,' said
Bridget. 'Not for us, but it is the beginning of the
new season, after all. We could have it while Gaylene's Hurtle is here, perhaps.'

'Do you mean so she could bring him along, or
in the hope that she would be otherwise occupied?'
enquired Calvin.

'The first, beast,' said Bridget. 'It's be-sweet-to-
Gaylene week this week, as far as I'm concerned.
All directed towards keeping the atmosphere pleasant for the production—I'm sure Owen will ap-
prove, won't you?'

'Oh—er—' said Owen, not certain whether irony
was intended.

'And, of course,' continued Bridget, 'towards
heaping coals of fire on Gaylene's head. The interesting thing will be how long it takes her to feel
the heat.'

But they were interrupted by Gaylene herself,
and a Gaylene who gave every indication of feeling
the heat. No one ever thought of her as a cool,
collected person, but they were all shocked to
silence by the image she presented today. She
threw open the main door, and strode forward.
Red, sweating, her flesh blotchy and her expression
vicious, she darted her bulbous eyes suspiciously
from one member of the little group to the other
as she came towards them. Suddenly there was no
longer anything funny about her: she had been
transformed from a comic gargoyle into a threatening figure of real menace, of a sort of malignant
power.

'All right,' she said. 'Who was it? Which of youse is trying to murder me?'

They had expected something melodramatic from her frightful appearance, but they hadn't expected that. There was complete silence among the group for several seconds, then someone shifted uneasily, and Raymond Ricci said: 'Oh, come off it, Gaylene—'

'Which was it?' bellowed Gaylene.

'Dear girl,' began Simon Mulley, 'let's talk this over rationally together—'

'None of that,' shouted Gaylene. 'I'm not in the mood for any of this at-heart-we're-all-good-pals stuff. I just want to know who did it.'

'If you were to tell us *what*,' suggested Bridget.

'Sneaked into my flat in the middle of the night and turned on my gas-fire, that's what. Any more questions?'

There was silence for a moment, and the little group seemed able to do no more than stand around and gape at her. On the one hand there was the natural tendency to treat the whole thing as a big farce—another of Gaylene's little ways, one which, like the rest, effectively drew attention to herself. On the other hand, that sweaty, bulging, shouting figure was horribly convincing: this looked like someone who really was beside herself with shock, rage and fear. Even Raymond Ricci piped down, though he was looking at her very closely, almost as if she were interesting from a dramatic point of view, a case-study. Finally Simon, as the oldest and most experienced in theatrical scenes, felt he had to say something.

'Really, Gaylene,' he began, trying to put a lot

of sympathy into his voice, 'can you be quite sure you didn't leave it on yourself, and it accidentally blew out?'

'On? In this heat? Are you crazy?'

'Or knocked it just before you went to bed?' suggested Calvin.

'I didn't go near the damned thing before I went to bed.' She turned aggressively on Calvin. 'Are you sure it wasn't you? You want me out of the company, that's for sure.'

'My dear girl, nobody wants you out of the company,' said Simon, an unfortunate lie that wouldn't for a moment get past Gaylene.

'Don't make me laugh,' she almost spat out. 'I'm the only first-rate voice in this company, and don't you all know it! Every one of you would pay my fare back to Australia like a shot, if you thought I'd go, and don't pretend you wouldn't. I suppose you hoped it would harm my voice?'

'You're being ridiculous, Gaylene,' said Raymond Ricci in that calm, suave voice of his.

'Oh, I hit the nail on the head, did I? You want to ruin my voice, do you? Well, let me tell you, you could have had a double murder on your hands!'

Double! Most of the company involuntarily looked towards Owen and then towards Ricci, and then realized with a start that if either of them had been with Gaylene last night, they would certainly have known about the gas-fire before now.

'I'm the last person to pry into your private life, Gaylene,' said Calvin eventually, 'but are you sure that—well, whoever you were with didn't turn on the gas? A sort of mutual suicide pact without your consent?'

'Funny bastard,' said Gaylene. 'Now listen here, you lot. I'm going to give this thing the works. I'm going to make sure the whole bloody company knows, and the newspapers as well. So if you've a mind to try these sneaky little tricks again, there'll be that much publicity you'll feel you've got the main spotlight on you.' She turned to Owen. 'And if you expect me to rehearse today, you've got another think coming. You can do without me. That's obviously somebody's aim—to do without me permanently!'

And Gaylene pranced out.

Her threat to tell the newspapers had caused a perceptible lowering of tension among the others. The hideous spectacle she had presented on her arrival, the spectacle of a rather unattractive animal at bay, combined with the passionate venom of her accusations, had convinced most of them that someone really had tried to kill Gaylene —or play a particularly nasty trick on her, at best. Each of them knew that they loathed her; most of them thought they knew that all or most of the others loathed her as well. This being so, they all had the fascinated, guilty feeling that what she said was not inherently improbable. But when she mentioned publicity—ah well: this was just Gaylene. Gaylene fed on newspaper items about herself. She was as hungry for a mention as a fading Hollywood actress or an up-and-coming politician. That explains things, they all told each other, in gestures and raisings of the eyebrow that

were more eloquent than words. Let's just forget it
and get back to work.

SINGER ACCUSES: SOMEONE IS TRYING TO KILL ME.
sang out the *Manchester Evening News.* Gaylene had given their reporter the works, and he
squeezed a picture of her, pop-eyed and malevo-
lent, on to the arts page. Other Northern journals
gave her a modicum of space, in the less serious
parts of the paper. The 'sensation' didn't last.
Stage-people are notoriously hysterical, suspicious,
prone to persecution mania. One couldn't pay attention to every one of them who made wild accusations of that sort, especially when the nation was
tottering from one financial brink to another, and
the football season was starting. The thing died
down.

In the company the gossip lasted a little longer.
The whisper went around that Gaylene's bed-
partner of the night in question had been Jim
McKaid, a small-part player with the company,
not much liked, with a chip on his shoulder and a
sense that managements 'held him back'. He had
a wife over in Dungannon, and he didn't want to
talk about the affair, but he did swap a few words
with Calvin while they were rehearsing the Second
Act, in which he played Marullo:

'She's a good lay all right,' he said, with his
twisted smile, 'but I'm damned if she's worth getting gassed for.'

# CHAPTER IV

## *Double Entry*

Giulia Contini, faithfully attended by her manager, Signor Pratelli, arrived from Verona on the Monday of the next week, and that evening they were entertained to cocktails by Mike Turner, the director, together with a group of notables—not members of the company, naturally, but local businessmen and civic dignitaries. The company, for its part, accepted that Mike had to go whoring after scraps of charity, and merely looked forward with anticipation to her appearance at the Friday morning rehearsal. She came late, of course. Mussolini was probably too busy making trains arrive on time to effect the same transformation on Italian singers—or if he did, his influence was as ephemeral as on the trains. Giulia was three-quarters of an hour late, and she came attended bustlingly by fat little Signor Pratelli, and by Mike, who smilingly ushered her in.

Visually, Signorina Contini was a great disappointment to Gaylene. She was short, plump, and quite unalluring, with a small, sharp-featured face that somehow managed to accommodate a good-humoured expression. She was, in fact, ordinary, as only an Italian girl can be ordinary, and the fact that she had bought most of her clothes from a good Italian couturier only underlined her ordinariness. The clothes had been the reward of success, and the success had been based on her winning the Bellini Competition in Siena the year before. Since then she had been much talked about in Italy, and her name had begun to penetrate to the outside world through reports in *Opera* and *The Times*. She had appeared in a mediocre Italian television production of *Madam Butterfly*, had been cheered rapturously at Rome, booed at Parma, and had cut her first disc of war-horses for Decca. The engagement with Northern Opera was her first modest excursion on to the international treadmill, and for this event she had expressed herself willing to learn the role in English. Her engagement in Manchester had aroused a little flutter of interest among English opera-goers, and before the first night she was to be interviewed by Alan Blyth.

Now, after she had divested herself of her splendid fur, which must have been prompted more by the *thought* of Manchester than by the actual climatic conditions that summer morning, she smiled around on her assembled fellow-singers with great geniality, and Mike took her protectively by the arm to effect introductions. Mike, a local boy made smooth, a little over-polite and always impeccably dressed, was nevertheless showing some small signs of nervousness. It soon became clear why.

'Buon giorno,' said Signorina Contini to the first singer Mike introduced her to. And then, waving her arms and saying something that sounded like 'No—I spick Ingliss!' she changed her greeting to

'Goo die'. It was all done with great good-humour, and Signor Pratelli, throughout the introductions, snuffled along in her wake, exuding concern and the Italian language. When the round of greetings had been made, Signorina Contini put down her handbag on a chair, looked around, and said: 'And then—what we does?'

The question gave Owen a chance to bustle forward and take charge, and perhaps to hide his uncertainty as to how he was going to deal with what looked like being an unexpectedly ticklish situation for him as producer.

'Well,' he said, 'we start with the Act 1 duets with Rigoletto, then those with the Duke—and in fact through to the end of the scene.'

'Ah, "*Caro nome*",' said Giulia. 'No—in Ingliss "Dearest nyme".'

'We're doing it in Italian, actually, for the first few rehearsals, to break you in, so to speak,' said Owen.

Giulia took some time to digest this, then she made a gesture of dismissal, and still with the same air of invincible good-humour, she said: 'No—is not necessary. I learns Ingliss for my career. I needs pracsis. We does in Ingliss.'

Owen was never happy when his decisions were not accepted without dispute, but when he opened his mouth to argue the matter, he saw Mike Turner making an infinitesimal gesture to him from the other side of the room, and he shut his mouth hurriedly again. It had been impressed very forcibly on Owen that his chances of further productions with the company depended on keeping the visiting star happy.

'OK, so be it—in English then,' he said. 'We'll take it from the end of *'Pari siamo'*. The pulpit steps are the stairs to your bedroom, Signorina Contini, and you come down those to welcome your father home.'

Giulia placed herself in the pulpit, and as Mr Pettifer finished Simon's soliloquy and the music pressed irresistibly forward for the entry of Gilda, she tripped down the stairs—tripping is something Italian sopranos can always do, at least until the pasta takes its toll—and ran to embrace Rigoletto.

'Gilda!' sang Simon Mulley.

'Ai-aa-a,' sang Giulia Contini.

'Daughter beloved! Thou art for me my only consolation,' sang Simon.

'Aa-er-ii-aa-er,' sang Giulia.

Mike Turner's face, safely behind Giulia's back, was a masterpiece of revealed emotion. It was the first big mistake of his directorship, but in the precarious position of the company very few mistakes could be allowed. And there was nothing anyone could do. It was too late to send Giulia for a crash course at the Berlitz School, and though Simon and Mr Pettifer very gently got together and made her say over her lines with the consonants inserted and the right sort of vowel sounds in the right places, any effect they had was quite transitory: after a line or so she went happily back to her glorious succession of odd-sounding diphthongs.

And it soon became clear that it wasn't just the words. Nobody except critics worries much about words. More than one international career has been built on a couple of vowel sounds. But the

voice was—a nice little voice: a sweet, mellifluous
instrument. A Mimi-voice.

The English singers in the hall had rather liked
their first view of Giulia Contini, but they would
have been less than human if they had not felt
some degree of insular satisfaction that the company already had in its midst a singer who could
sing rings round the visiting star as Gilda—or for
that matter as Mimi, or as anything else. Gaylene's
emotions, of course, were more mixed. She had
been hoping that the arrival of Signorina Contini
would knock all this Bridget-worship on the head,
once and for all. *That* clearly wasn't going to happen. On the other hand, no singer, least of all
Gaylene, could resist a slight spasm of satisfaction
if a fellow-artist turned out to be less talented than
he had been cracked up to be.

'I'm *still* the only first-rate voice in the company,' she said in a loud whisper to Jim McKaid,
who gave her the vitriolic look of an acknowledged
second-rate voice.

Acting-wise, things hardly went any better. Nobody expects Italian singers to be able to act, and
Owen had looked forward to imposing his ideas
on Giulia, to wrenching some sort of a performance
out of her. So he was not worried by her tiny repertoire of vague supplicatory gestures of the left
hand, her clappings of the bosom with the right,
the little bends at the knees before high notes. To
drill into her a series of movements and gestures
which would be a substitute for a real dramatic
rendering of the part would be a great satisfaction
to Owen. And he did indeed get somewhere mo-

mentarily when he tried to stop her looking continually and fixedly in the direction of the imaginary audience.

'Where I look?' said Giulia equably.

'Look at your father,' said Owen.

'Oo?' said Giulia.

'Your father. Rigoletto.'

'Oh—'im,' said Giulia, and for the space of two seconds she looked mooningly at Simon, before turning back to the inevitable audience.

Later in the duet, though, he met with more determined resistance. At the climax of the duet he asked her, as he had Bridget, to clasp her hands.

'What?' said Giulia.

'Clasp your hands,' said Owen, showing her.

Giulia looked at him intently, tentatively intertwined her fingers, essayed a few notes, and then said: 'I no clasp my 'ands.'

Owen's voice, in spite of all his care, rose a fraction.

'Will you please try it for this rehearsal?' he asked.

'I no clasp my 'ands,' said Giulia flatly.

For a moment Owen completely forgot who he was talking to, let the blood rush to his head, and let out the first tiny beginnings of a shout. Just in time he registered from the other side of the hall Mike Turner, whose gesturing was now much more obvious, and he also caught some Italian from Signor Pratelli which he took to mean 'She no clasp 'er 'ands.' He got a grip on himself, and let the rehearsal go forward.

Calvin and Giulia did a pretty love-duet. Calvin was determined to show Gaylene that passion was not only to be expressed through sweaty clinches, so the passion he put into this duet was elegant, light, but full of feeling. Rehearsing with Bridget had helped, and perhaps watching Raymond Ricci with his succession of girl-friends over the past year had contributed something too, for whatever one thought about his morals, Raymond had a certain style. Giulia responded prettily but phlegmatically, and the frenzied success of 'Addios' that concluded the duet turned out comic rather than impassioned. Then Giulia ran through 'Caro nome'—nicely, pathetically, with a generalized Puccinian emotion which was not quite what Verdi wanted. She ended with a trill that was little more than a vocal shiver. Then she let herself be abducted with the usual token resistance—a couple of kicks—and the scene ended with Jim McKaid making little of the hopeless part of Marullo, and Simon trying rather desperately to restore some dramatic life to things with the discovery that his daughter had gone.

'Very nice, for a first run-through,' said Owen, with quite uncharacteristic diplomacy.

Gaylene, less of a diplomat, but more of a liar, went straight over to Giulia, took her by the arm in a gesture that said 'we are the stars of this performance', and said: 'Nice to hear a voice with body to it. That's a real lovely sound you make.'

Giulia looked as if she did not know quite what to make of this, or even who this was, and merely murmured: 'Grazie.'

'I'm hoping we're going to be able to put a bit of life into this production between us,' continued Gaylene unperturbed. 'They're terribly inhibited

this lot—they can't *give*, know what I mean? I
hope we'll be able to give things a bit of *go*.'

'Gow?' said Giulia, frowning in bewilderment.
Then, as if she took the word as an order, she detached herself from Gaylene's elephantine confidentiality, and drifted off.

Gaylene looked at her exasperatedly, and then
with that rapid and complete change from one
transparent emotion to another which was charac-
teristic of her, she smiled in anticipated triumph,
looked at her watch, and said: 'Hell, it's nearly
twelve. I've got to go and get Hurtle.'

As she made towards the door, Mike Turner
looked in her direction perplexedly and said: 'She's
got to go and get *what*?' as though she had uttered
an Australian obscenity he hadn't heard before.

'Hurtle,' said Calvin. 'We gather it's a name.
He's her boy-friend, or fiancé or something.'

'I don't know that I like her bringing him along
without so much as by-your-leave,' said Owen.

'Give us a break,' said Calvin. 'We're all dying
to see the lucky guy. You stop her and you'll have
an industrial dispute on your hands that will make
Lord Harewood's troubles look like the Teddy-
bears' picnic.'

Giulia, meanwhile, had settled into a corner with
Bridget, and together they were going through the
English words of the part of Gilda. Bridget had
enough Italian—albeit of a somewhat operatic,
melodramatic kind—to fill in the gaps, the frequent
gaps, where Giulia's English failed, and she got
some really useful work done. Within ten minutes
they were bosom friends, in the manner of theatre
people, and Giulia was insisting that she do a dem-

onstration. The difficult phrase was 'he awoke my first desire', a phrase in 'Caro nome' which led to another rising phrase with a succession of trills which made the words particularly difficult to integrate into the vocal line. Bridget resisted for a time, with a realistic awareness of the strength of theatrical intimacies. Finally, after much solicitation, and thinking 'this is the end of a beautiful friendship', she closed her eyes and opened up.

'He awoke my first desire'

On the first note the rest of the hall went silent. Bridget was in particularly full, opulent voice. The trills were real trills, and they were miraculously well-placed and true. Now she'd done it, everybody thought. They waited for a reaction. As she finished, Giulia opened her eyes wide in pure pleasure.

'Beautiful,' she cried. 'Is wonderful. *Incredible.* You go on, please go on.'

Everyone was terribly disappointed. In spite of her protests, Bridget was forced to sing the next few phrases, taking the high notes at the return of the phrase 'caro nome' with swelling panache. Giulia took her hands in a gesture more uninhibitely operatic than anything she had produced during the rehearsal, kissed her on both cheeks, and said: 'Is a great voice. You be a great star!'

Signor Pratelli did not look too pleased, but everyone else had to admit that Giulia was either an unexpectedly good off-stage actress, or else a very nice girl indeed.

Everyone, that is, except Gaylene.

She had made an entrance two minutes before, with Hurtle in tow, and had watched the scene

with anger and contempt. She contemplated push-
ing him out to make a second one, but deciding he
would probably not be cooperative, she was forced
to shove her way forward, dragging a sheepish
Hurtle by the arm, and bellowing round: 'Hey, this
is my bloke.'

After that, there didn't seem much chance of
any meaningful rehearsal that day. Gaylene, on the
way to the bus stop to pick up Hurtle, had
equipped herself with a leaning tower of paper
cups and five bottles of an Australian red wine
which was probably designed to show the Italian
what real quality wine tasted like. As she took
Hurtle from person to person, introducing each one
as if they were the best friend she had in the
world, she handed them a cup and said: 'Be round
in two ticks with the booze.'

'This was meant to be a rehearsal, you know,
Gaylene,' said Mike Turner.

'Stiff-necked lot,' yelled Gaylene. 'Well, now it's
meant to be a party.'

Hurtle was a little apologetic about it all. He was
a very large young man, in his mid-twenties, with
a face set in an expression of imperturbable good-
humour, only momentarily crossed by flickers of
embarrassment at the proprietorial behaviour of
Gaylene. Real life, for Hurtle, it seemed, began
when the whistle went and play commenced. What
happened off the field was a jolly game which he
was quite prepared to amble through with great
amiability, hoping that no one tried to take it seriously, or pretended that anything that happened
beyond the touch-lines mattered in any way.

'Jeez, Gay, I'm in training,' he said, when she filled his paper cup with Penfold's.

'I should hope so,' said Gaylene. 'And I don't mean for football, either.'

From then on the rehearsal became an impromptu party, and Gaylene playing the hostess was a sight to behold. She charged around with noisy gaiety, bellowing to people to enjoy themselves, clinking paper cups in cheery toasts and shouting 'skoal' and 'bottoms up' to everyone in sight. Hurtle bumbled along in her wake for a bit, like a cowed dog, but when she had told people for the sixteenth time that he was 'the best damned scrum-half in Australia,' and had explained to him for the tenth time that you had to call it 'rugby' in this country, because 'football is soccer, would you believe it?' he showed a surprising nimbleness, and got out of her way, eventually ambling over in the direction of Bridget and Calvin.

'Awfully lucky, your playing here while Gaylene is with the company,' said Bridget, smiling.

'Oh, Gay always manages to turn up somewhere or other,' said Hurtle. 'No getting away from Gay.'

'Have you known each other long?' asked Calvin.

'Jeez yes,' said Hurtle. 'We were both at Coonabarrabran High. She was just Gay French then—with the ordinary old single capital F. We used to train together.'

'Train?'

'Gay was a great little hurdler, and a pretty good gymnast. She always had this weight problem, and she wouldn't diet, so she never made the grade, but she was real neat.'

'I would have made the grade too,' bellowed Gaylene, who was yards away, but had long ears. 'I just chose to concentrate on my singing instead.'

'Poor old Gay,' said Hurtle, turning back to Bridget and Calvin, 'she never could bear to come second. Good job, really, she gave up: she'd have turned the Olympic Games into World War III.'

'How long have you been engaged?' said Bridget.

'Engaged?'

'Well, if Gay says so, that's OK by me,' said Hurtle with a look of unquenchable good-humour.

'I suppose you'll be hoping Gaylene could get in with the Elizabethan Theatre Trust,' said Calvin. 'So you could be together.'

'Together?'

'When you're married.'

'Oh gee,' said Hurtle with a grin. 'I don't know as I'd go that far.'

Gaylene had caught the reference to the Elizabethan Theatre Trust, and pushed her way over.

'I can go back t'Australia any time I like,' she said. 'They've been putting out feelers for months.' (She made it sound uniquely indecent.) 'As a matter of fact I'm expecting a call any day now to the Sydney Opera House.'

'Why, do they need someone to prop up the sails?' said Hurtle, with a splendid, braying laugh.

'Big joke, scunge,' said Gaylene, giving him the sort of shove that would have sent a lesser man through the wall. But she seemed to put up with a lot more from Hurtle than she would from any other of her boy-friends. Perhaps it was the softening influence of their shared school-days.

As the party wore on, and Gaylene became more

imaginatively boastful, Hurtle became confidential with those he talked to.

'You don't want to take Gay too seriously,' he said to Simon Mulley, who was watching him closely, as if studying him for some role in comic opera.

'Oh, we don't,' Simon said.

'Mostly, you see, she just says the first thing that comes into her head,' said Hurtle.

'Yes, we realize that,' said Simon. He added, since Hurtle seemed so notably unbesotted a lover: 'We just wish the first things were pleasanter than they usually are.'

'Jeez, don't we all?' said Hurtle. 'Of course, you've got to take a lot of what she says with a pinch of salt, you know.'

'Yes—actually we had noticed that too,' said Simon.

'But there's no harm in her,' said Hurtle.

'No,' said Simon, and Hurtle caught the faintest hint of a rising, interrogative intonation.

'Wouldn't hurt a fly,' he said earnestly. 'Provided it didn't get in her way.'

At the other end of the hall Gaylene was speculating about her future prospects. A little group had collected around her, for singers are fascinated by other singers' lies and fantasies, and can never quite rid themselves of the fear that they might be true.

'Tell you the truth,' Gaylene said, 'I'm not sure I'll go back to Sydney, not for a while yet anyways. You can't really build an international career with Sydney as a base. And they're mad to get me at the English National, you know.'

'Really?' said Raymond Ricci at his suavest. 'What's holding them back?'

'There's a lot of professional jealousy in the company,' said Gaylene. 'Among that drack lot of mezzos—natch. Some people don't like healthy competition. But there's a tremendous *claque* building up for me in the gallery.'

'The Earl's Court Yobboes,' said Jim McKaid. 'Lord Harewood would rather die than give way to that sort of mob.'

'Or rather *you* died,' said Raymond. 'That's an idea, you know. Can't you just imagine Lord Harewood popping over from Harewood House, creeping up your darkened stairs that night, picking your lock, and turning on your gas-fire? No? Well, maybe not. Still, it's a possibility to bear in mind.'

'I'm surprised about being engaged to Gay,' said Hurtle, sitting on the pulpit stairs and speaking a little tipsily, for he didn't often break training, and the wine packed a thoroughly nasty punch. 'I'd have thought she'd've got over that.'

'Got over it?' said Owen, looking at Hurtle uncertainly.

'She always used to do it—back at Coona in the last year at High. Got engaged regularly once a week. Used to march into class and announce it on Monday mornings, regular as clockwork. But eventually even Gay had to see the funny side of that.'

Owen gave a wintry smile.

'I'm surprised she's taken it up again,' said Hurtle, with confused confidentiality. 'Is she having trouble getting chaps?'

'I—er—believe not,' said Owen.

'That's a relief,' said Hurtle. 'You never know

with these stage people, do you? Eventually she'll get desperate, but I hope that'll be when I'm not around. I'd give her a couple of years or so yet, so I'll have time to take cover.'

'Hurtle,' boomed a voice like the noon-day gun from the other side of the hall.

'What is it, Gay?' said Hurtle.

'They're getting at me,' said Gaylene. Finally the insults had penetrated through her drunken good-humour, and she looked purple and angry.

'Take it easy, Gay,' said Hurtle, strolling over. 'You always play in the scrum—in there shoving and kicking. Why don't you make for the outfield now and then?'

'Take me home,' commanded Gaylene. 'It's nearly four. I need something inside me.'

'Is Australians always so beeg?' said Giulia Contini to Bridget, as she watched their cinemascoped figures heading for the door.

'Always,' said Bridget. 'The race has expanded to fill the available space.'

But Gaylene and Hurtle were interrupted in their departure. At the door there appeared a diminutive chap with a worried expression on his face. He looked about twelve, but in fact he was an unemployed school-leaver whom Mike Turner paid tiny sums to do odd jobs around the theatre.

'I've got a message from Mr Turner,' he said.

'Mike?' said Gaylene. 'Isn't he here?'

'Naw,' said the boy. ''E's been back at the theatre for hours. Which one is Bridget?'

'There,' said Gaylene, pointing sourly.

''E says, do you know the part of . . . Fordlingi,' said the boy to Bridget.

'Of *what*?'

'Ee, I've got it written down 'ere,' said the boy, handing her a scrap of paper.

'Fiordiligi,' said Bridget. 'Yes, I sang it at college.'

'Well, there's one gone sick,' said the boy, "er as was in't family way. And 'e wants you to sing tomorrow.'

'Christ,' said Gaylene, clutching Hurtle in an iron grip, and making off with him through the door. 'Now we really are down to Amateur Night at the RSL.'

# CHAPTER V

*One Fine Day*

It is not often hot in Manchester. When it is, the air is laden, the atmosphere almost tangible, and the warmth and grime and buzz of activity combine to exhaust the most active, to make people pant for rest and relief.

It was a stifling day of this sort in early September that sent Calvin out into the park to sunbathe, to idle through the papers, and to think of Bridget. He was purposely keeping out of her way, for she had only this one morning and afternoon of rehearsal before appearing in *Così Fan Tutte* at 7:30. Even for a more experienced singer the prospect would be daunting. The day before, after receiving the summons, she had kissed him and retreated to her flat to study the score with that fierce concentration and energy which he recognized as part of her distinction as a singer. Today she would be rehearsing, working through her moves, establishing her relationships with the other characters. He knew she would want to be free of any distraction, particularly any emotional distraction. She would not want his advice: they discussed their parts, but in the end what they did was based on lonely personal decisions. It had to be so. And particularly now, with only one day's notice, he realized instinctively that Bridget's Fiordiligi would be the result of a hard white flame of concentration. So he would leave her alone, and slip into the gallery in the evening.

He lay, lazy in the grimy sun, thinking about how the rehearsal would be going, thinking about himself, about his roles, about his future. He smiled sleepily to himself as he thought how these things always shifted and coalesced: when he played Rodolfo he could never keep Bridget out of his mind; when he was with Bridget he could never quite forget how he played Rodolfo. Perhaps it was a good thing that, as a tenor, he never got to play roles of any great psychological complexity. Tenors loved and died. He wished he was playing Ferrando to Bridget's Fiordiligi: that was a part for him—light, sweet, impassioned. He tried over a phrase from 'Un aura amorosa', much to the surprise of a shop-girl taking an early lunch-break, who had been lying near him and looking at his brown baking body with interest, but who now put him down as a screwball.

The sun ate into him, fighting against the particles of dust and smoke, and he lay, making patterns of his future, of the roles he would sing, and the houses he would sing in. Glyndebourne had been showing a tentative interest: he could expect small roles first, then bigger. Could he do the Rossini tenor roles? Yes, he thought he could. And Donizetti and Bellini. The bigger parts would have to wait. The voice would grow, he was sure of that, but he must not force it. The operatic world was littered with the blasted careers of tenors who forced their voices. Present and future, dream and reality merged in a hazy, warm, comfortable meditation.

Opening an eye, preparatory to turning over on to his stomach he blinked, and registered among the dressed and undressed Mancunians around him in the park figures that he knew. He blinked again, and shook the sun from his head. Standing over in the shade of a clump of trees was the lithe, saturnine figure of Raymond Ricci, dressed as usual in black—incongruous in the summer heat, and adding to his suave, Mephistophelean air. He was bending his great height over—who? The girl turned round, looking the length of the park, and he saw it was Giulia Contini. She was wearing a dull grey skirt and a nondescript blue sweater. Calvin was puzzled. What had those two to say to each other that demanded an interview in the middle of the park? Was Ricci adding another to his long list of conquests? Surely Signor Pratelli would guard his charge better than that? He could see that Giulia, though decidedly uninteresting physically, would be an attractive proposition for the limpet type. She would be raking in the money, for the next two or three years at least, and a star-quality soprano could always insist on engagements with her less than star-quality husband. Was Raymond Ricci the limpet type? Calvin turned the question lazily over in his mind for a little.

Then a more comfortable idea occurred to him. Of course, Raymond was virtually an Italian. He spoke it like a native. Naturally Giulia would welcome the chance to talk freely with him—as a rest

from busy, voluble little Signor Pratelli. As he lux-
uriously turned himself over, he thought he noticed
Giulia was gesturing emphatically, and that her
face looked troubled, but he settled his face down
on his folded shirt, closed his eyes, and felt the
sun seep into his grassy back.

Raymond Ricci strolled through the traffic and the
hot, irritable shoppers towards the stage door, with
that catlike tread that was going to be so effective
in the part of Sparafucile. His eyelids were sta-
tioned at their usual position of two-thirds down
his eyeballs, and his face was lazily impassive. Only
he could know that the muscles at the side of his
mouth were twitching, in the beginnings of a
smile. Raymond was pleased with himself.

As he pushed open the stage-door casually, he
registered at once Harrison, the stage-door-keeper.
Sergeant Harrison to the performers of the Northern Opera, and to the young people in the gallery
of the Prince of Wales Theatre, whom he ruled
with a rod of iron and berated with a voice of
sounding brass on his rare visits to that casual,
carefree and good-hearted extremity of the theatre.
Sergeant Harrison of the square build, Sergeant
Harrison of the Chaplin moustache, Sergeant Harrison of the heavy hand, formed for raising a pint
mug or smacking bottoms. Raymond Ricci noticed
that Sergeant Harrison was being polite. Sergeant
Harrison was not always polite, either to the
greater or the lesser stars under his ex-regimental
supervision.

'Mr Ritchie, thank 'eavens you've cum,' he said
'There's this telegram cum for you.'

He passed the telegram over, and thoughts went through Ricci's mind of his father, frailer than he ought to be, from over-work, and of his fat, cheery mother. Ripping it open he registered at once it had nothing to do with them. It was from abroad. Oslo. The words 'Don Giovanni' and 'tonight' hit him in the face at once. This was the second time this had happened: he'd been called to Lyons to sing the same part in March, and there had been a complimentary note in Opera. Now Oslo. All on the strength of a few performances with the Glyndebourne Touring Company. Not bad. Of course, Don Giovannis didn't grow on trees, that was the reason, but still—not bad. It was a chance. A rush of thoughts went through Ricci's head, a series of blinding explosions. It was a chance, a possibility, an unlooked-for opportunity.

'Get on the phone to the airport,' he said to Sergeant Harrison. 'With a bit of luck there'll be a plane that will make it in time.'

Owen Caulfield and Simon Mulley were alone with Mr Pettifer for one of the last Rigoletto rehearsals in the Pitford Methodist Hall. Already some rehearsals had taken place at the Prince of Wales Theatre, and tomorrow was to see the first full-scale rehearsal there with orchestra, costumes and scenery: they were into the last, exciting phase that would culminate in the dress rehearsal and the first night. The Methodist Hall would then be given over to other singers, rehearsing other works.

Throughout the afternoon the two men had jogged along as best they could. Owen knew that

with Simon Mulley he had to use the velvet glove,
but there never was a velvet glove that more pat-
ently revealed the would-be iron hand inside. The
worst of it was that with part of his conscious
mind Owen had to admit that Simon had a real
psychological grasp, and that, as a born man of
the theatre, he knew precisely the most economical means to convey his perceptions. But Owen
fought the admission: his own personal uncer-
tainties made it almost impossible for him to admit
brain, or talent, or potential in others. They were
objects, to be manipulated, wheedled, bullied.

Simon, for his part, wrestled with his role, went
through the difficult phrases with Mr Pettifer over
and over again, and all the time watched Owen.
He tried to work with him, tried to integrate his
suggestions into his performance, tried to discuss
and compromise. But all the time he watched him,
as if sparks from that difficult, twisted personality
were to light the fire of his own performance as
Rigoletto.

'I feel it's working against the music, dear boy,'
Simon said finally, after Owen had tried to impose
on him a series of stereotyped dramatic gestures
for Rigoletto's big scene with the courtiers in
Act II. 'Of course it has to be theatrical to a certain
extent, but you've also got to realize that this is
the most terrible thing that has ever happened to
him: the man's distraught, off his head with hatred
and fear and contempt. We can't rely on the same
old gestures to get this across.'

Owen was really annoyed. He hadn't thought of
the moves he had been suggesting to Simon as
being 'the same old gestures'. Coming from a man

with over a hundred performances of Rigoletto to his credit, the comment was damning. Nor did anything else more psychologically revealing suggest itself to him. He swallowed hard, twice.

'Well,' he said. 'Let's run through the whole scene again, and do it your way. OK?'

They went through the whole scene, from the courtiers' taunting of Rigoletto, through his furious outburst 'Cortigiani, vil razza dannata', to the pleading and self-pity with which this part of the scene concludes. Simon Mulley was not a tall man, or a particularly striking one in everyday life, in spite of the touch of theatricality in his manner, but as soon as he opened his mouth he fixed the attention, so that the eye caught and the mind saw the significance of every tiny gesture. He succeeded in creating the entire scene: the courtiers, led by Marullo; the air of decadent elegance; the bile and heartbreak of Rigoletto himself. His gestures were taut, but they suggested a personality close to the end of his tether. Only in the final appeal did the innate theatricality of the jester, the side of him that was constantly giving a performance, break out in broad gestures of supplication. Whether or not it was intended as such, it was a lesson to Owen.

Owen let a moment or two elapse.

'Well, of course, if that's how you feel it . . .' he said. Then, with a little struggle, he added: 'There were some fine moments. I'll have to rethink the courtiers' movements, but I needn't worry you with that. Now, could we run through 'Pari siamo' just once more, do you think?'

They started in on the crucial monologue of self-doubt and self-disgust. When Simon came to the line: 'That old man laid his curse on me', he put his hand to his breast in a gesture of terror and foreboding. Owen stopped Mr Pettifer.

'Very theatrical, don't you feel, Simon?'

Simon Mulley understood now why Owen had wanted to go over '*Pari siamo*' again. He always made this gesture at this point, and Owen had felt the need to score off him after his implied criticism of the standardized theatricality of his own suggested movements.

'But at this point there *is* a touch of theatricality,' Simon explained patiently. 'He's superstitious and afraid, but nothing has happened yet. He's a man who spends his life performing, so it's natural to him to exaggerate a little.' Then, unwisely, he added: 'Listen to the music, dear boy; always listen to the music. That will tell you.'

If there was anything Owen disliked more than people who disputed his orders, it was people who gave him advice. The first brought his judgement into question, but the second cast doubt on his whole competence to do his job.

'Will you, just for once, Simon, let me do my own job without offering little dribs and drabs of platitudinous advice?' he said, in a high strident voice. 'You're not the only one in this company who knows how to listen to music.' He glared, red and furious, at the company's star.

'I'm sure Mr Mulley was only trying to be helpful,' put in Mr Pettifer nervously from the piano.

'The most helpful thing he could do would be to put his own performance in order, instead of reeling from one style of acting to another,' continued Owen relentlessly. 'God only knows how I am supposed to fit this mish-mash of mannerisms in with the rest of the production.'

'Most of the rest of the cast are musicians,' said Simon with no attempt to disguise his contempt. 'You will find we shall not have any trouble. Could we take it from the beginning, Mr Pettifer?'

He turned towards an imaginary audience a long way away from where Owen was standing and sang the opening lines:

'We are equals . . . He is the man of laughter,
        and I of murder.'

Both the others noticed that he had inadvertently got them the wrong way round.

The house for the first night of the revival of *Così Fan Tutte* was not quite full. There had been several performances the previous season, *Così* being a suitably small-scale opera for a company that had to watch every penny. The stifling weather, too, may have kept some of the more expensive seats unfilled, though the gallery was full of young people, some in jeans, some in shorts, many in love. Among the last was Calvin, sitting alone, and tense with anticipation. Before the lights went down Mike Turner made the announcement that Bridget was substituting for the ailing and pregnant soprano originally scheduled. The news caused no particular disappointment or expectation. Oddly enough, though, from the first bars of the overture some of the habitual galleryites no-

ticed that the orchestra was playing with a zing, an
effervescence, which had been definitely lacking in
the performances last season. And from the moment the two ladies entered and floated their
voices into an amorous concerted cadenza, there
was a hush in the gallery, and an exchanging of
meaningful glances that somehow communicated
itself to the rest of the house, so that a thrill of
expectation—expectation of quite what nobody
knew—settled itself on stalls and balcony. And
backstage as well, where the undersized teenager
who had fetched her the previous day was watching Bridget from the wings with an expression
which could denote nothing but calf-love.

Bridget felt the expectation. She had been rehearsing in the heat all day, and if she thought
about it she would probably be tired. She did not
think about it. She thought only of giving enough
voice, but not too much—enough to reach the gallery, not so much as to coarsen the tone. Hellish
difficult in a new theatre, and one so different from
the little college theatre where she had played the
part before. A devil of a part, too: one couldn't
skimp on the acting side and concentrate on the
singing. This was one opera where everything had
to be totally integrated, or the whole thing fell
flat. The test would come at 'Come scoglio.'

When 'Come scoglio' came, Bridget had got the
feel of the stage and the measure of the theatre,
and was beginning to feel in total control of herself. If only the voice comes good, she said to
herself. That fearsome extension down to the very
lowest range of the voice, those ridiculous leaps.
A voice that has been singing Gilda for some

weeks was not really prepared. And the fire, the storm, the passion—how would they come?

As Bridget turned to her pseudo-Albanian lover to launch her long, indignant recitative, she suddenly thought of Gaylene. Of Gaylene in the Methodist Hall turning on her, furious with jealousy, and screaming: 'He's black!' Bridget squared her shoulders, and, fortified by the horrid memory, launched her fury at the stolid, rather lethargic frame of the tenor playing Ferrando. He looked as though he didn't quite know what was hitting him.

As the aria proper began Bridget turned to the audience. She was proclaiming her utter fidelity, blazoning her chastity to the roof-tops. 'Like a rock,' she trumpeted, 'in ocean planted!' The leaps came confidently, the lower notes firm, full, implacably determined. Out there somewhere, she knew, Calvin must be sitting. She sang to him. The rich, creamy sound surged out into the auditorium, sending shivers of sensuous pleasure down spines in the back row of the gallery. As the aria speeded up to its conclusion Bridget turned back to her sheepish, lumpish tenor, and fixed him with a blazing eye. Scorn, rejection, unutterable aversion were written in every line of her face.

She was thinking of Gaylene. As the voice thrilled out in a virtuoso display of fireworks she was thinking of Gaylene—sweaty, red, and screaming that day in the Methodist Hall: 'He's a nigger. He's a bloody black!'

She was seeing Gaylene in her mind's eye, but ironically enough the lady herself was at that moment in the theatre, looking not unlike President

Amin after he has been left by one of his wives.
She was standing in the gangway along the back
of the gallery, her eyes bulging, her face shining
with sweat, and with anger, jealousy and contempt
oozing out of every pore. As the orchestra brought
the aria to a close, and a great bray of triumphal,
hysterical appreciation burst from the lusty young
lungs of the gallery, she turned and shoved her
way violently through the swing doors to the stairs.

Sergeant Harrison was standing by the door. He
didn't know much about opera, but he was man of
the theatre enough to have scented an approach-
ing triumph several minutes before, and had crept
in to be part of it. He was also man of the theatre
enough to recognize professional jealousy when he
saw it. Watching Gaylene's departure, he smiled to
himself a little smile of recognition.

Gaylene barged through the gallery door to the
street, her eyes and mouth set hard. To the casual
observer she looked thoroughly disagreeable: to
anyone who knew her better she looked menacing.
She marched straight ahead down the centre of
the pavement, and policemen and dockers in her
path moved cautiously aside. She commandeered
a bus, and slapped her fare into the conductor's
hand. When she reached the old Victorian house
which included her own flat, she tramped up the
long staircase with a heavy, even, measured stomp,
and banged the flat door behind her. She strode
to the kitchen cupboard, poured out a half-tum-
blerful of whisky, splashed a dash of tap-water in
it, and began sluicing it around her large mouth
in venomous meditation.

One and a half hours later she was feeling and looking (though not smelling) a lot better. She was meeting Hurtle for an after-match supper at the Bristol, and she had put on a bright pink dress, very low-cut, and leaving to the imagination only the question of how it was kept up. Above the great expanse of brawny shoulders and fleshy arms her face had been well painted to hide the effects of drink and rage. Her long black hair had been slapped magisterially into place, and sprayed there, and her feet were decked out in gold, spangly evening sandals. All in all, she felt she looked good. Manchester didn't deserve her. But then, nor had Coonabarrabran.

She looked around the flat, and turned off the light. She felt for the switch to the light on the stairs, and clicked it. Nothing happened.

'Damn,' she boomed in a voice that reached down to the occupants of the flat below. 'Bloody landlord!'

She hitched up her skirt and trod gingerly on the top stair. Then she clomped heavily on to the next, and with added confidence on to the next and the next. At the fifth step the elderly couple downstairs heard the regular thuds of her descent being succeeded by a slither, a bellow, and a succession of thumps, and finally a sound like a ton of coal reaching the floor of an exceptionally deep coal-hole. When they opened their door and let the light flood out on to the landing, they saw a great heap of pink silk, red flesh and gold lamé, and a pair of bright, vicious eyes.

'Christ in Hell,' roared Gaylene. 'They nearly got me that time.'

# CHAPTER VI

*La Commedia E Finita*

It was Thursday 7 September. Ten o'clock in the morning.

Gaylene Ffrench woke gradually, but did not open her eyes. She pulled the sheet and blanket well over her face, but she felt over to the other side of the double bed. Her hand met nothing until it reached the far side of the mattress. Under the bedclothes Gaylene's lower lip protruded itself in a pout.

Ten minutes later she rose and walked a little uncertainly towards the bathroom. Fifteen minutes later the door opened agtin, and steam, an over-powering smell of body-lotion, and Gaylene emerged. She had nothing on. The curtains of her living-room were not drawn, and Gaylene glanced surreptitiously towards the offices of a small insurance company on the other side of the street. Someone was in the window, looking at her. Gaylene smiled to herself and went towards the kitchen to cook her breakfast.

One plate of sausage, bacon, kidney, mushroom and egg and two slices of toast and honey later Gaylene went to her wardrobe and stood before it in meditation. It was the first rehearsal at the

Prince of Wales Theatre. Costume would be worn,
but since Gaylene did not appear until the last
act, she would be sitting around criticizing the
others for much of the time. She selected a tight,
shiny dress, quite unsuitable for her figure and for
the weather. She walked through the living-room
to the big mirror in the hall, all the time keeping
half an eye on the window of the insurance office
across the street. She peered into the mirror and
inspected a bluish bruise on the left side of her
face. Then she looked at her hair. It was a mess.
She made experimental dabs at it with pudgy
fingers and grimaced. She reached for the phone,
seized it with her large hand and took it with her
into the living-room. She perched on the side of
an armchair, always with half an eye on the
houses opposite. She rang her hairdresser and
asked him if she could be fitted in that morning—
or rather told him that she could. She did not
notice any ambiguities in the tone of his assent.

'Be there in twenty minutes flat,' she said, and
slammed the telephone down.

Then she stood in the middle of the living-room
and slipped on the dress she had selected. And
very little else. She slapped powder and cream on
her face, paying particular attention to the bruise
on the left side. She drew a vivid red line around
her great mouth, and admired the forties-era sexi-
ness about her preferred shiny brand of lipstick.
Now she seemed to be ready. She took up a plastic
bag, in which she had placed fruit and cakes, and
took a last look round the flat. She opened the
front door, switched on the staircase light, fixed
now, and descended the stairs without mishap.

When she reached the street she registered a face
or two in the office, now above her, but she con-
trived to give the impression of complete uncon-
sciousness as she turned right and swaggered up
the street. People looked at her, and turned to look
at her again. If she had had the right mechanism,
she would have purred.

Arriving at the hairdressers' she at once took
over the shop. She commandeered a place and demanded the attention of her favourite assistant.
She was one of the establishment's better-known
clients, and was allowed to do what she wanted.
She sent out for all available Northern papers, and
gave directions about what to do with her hair.
She talked loudly, and in the manner of people
who do not need to give a second thought to the
question of whether or not shop-assistants and
other menials hate them. Among the girls behind
the chairs some glances passed, but nothing was
said.

'Never known it so hot, have you?' said the
assistant who had been chosen to attend to Gaylene's hair.

'You call this hot?' said Gaylene scornfully. 'This
is a cool day where I come from.'

From this truth she proceeded to certain other
comparisons between Australia and Great Britain,
not all based so securely on fact, but all utterly
to the detriment of the latter country. The assistant showed every sign of thinking her own
thoughts.

The papers arrived, and Gaylene snatched them
without a word of thanks. At last she shut up, and
her fingers worked their way feverishly through

the pages. Towards the back of the *Manchester Globe* she found what she wanted. A smile lit up her heavy face, and she opened the paper up to get a better look.

'That's me,' she said to the assistant.

The picture showed Gaylene and Hurtle eating their evening meal at the Bristol the night before. Underneath there was a short paragraph headed ' "They've tried again," says Soprano'. The inaccurate description of her voice did not seem to worry Gaylene. She gazed at the picture with infinite self-satisfaction.

'I like your dress,' said the assistant.

'Cost a packet,' said Gaylene complacently.

'Your boy-friend looks nice,' said the girl sincerely. 'I like the cheery type, don't you?'

Gaylene's glance strayed for the first time to the beaming face of Hurtle. It seemed to consort ill with the story under the picture. The smile left her face.

'Bloody fool sometimes,' she said.

She riffled through the rest of the papers. Two of them contained tiny paragraphs on the incident of the night before. Gaylene read them with signs of only a very moderate satisfaction. Then she settled down in the chair to contemplate in the mirror her own physical perfection.

A moment later a thought seemed to occur to her. She jerked herself up, to the irritation of her hairdresser, and grabbed the *Guardian*. She turned to the Arts Page. In the far right-hand column there was a long review headed 'A Glorious Debut'.

The assistant had never seen anybody snarl before. She saw it now. If it hadn't been one of the things frowned on in Coonabarrabran Gaylene would have spat. She read on:

> The Northern Opera Company has attracted a great many talented young singers to Lancashire, but last night it created its first star. Bridget Lander, a last-minute replacement, had the Prince of Wales Theatre in the palm of her hand from her first entry, and by the end of the evening there was cheering and applause such as can seldom have been heard in Manchester even for the visiting London companies. It was well-deserved: the voice is full, well-controlled and quite exceptionally beautiful. It is used with an artistry extraordinary in one of Miss Lander's years. Her acting was at first rudimentary, but it gained in confidence as the evening progressed. This is a splendid performance of Fiordiligi, and is on the way to becoming a great one. In the part of Ferrando, Robert Harshaw was less remarkable . . .

It appeared that the sun had gone in for Gaylene. She sat, frowning and sulking, and the hairdresser's great mirror reflected every shade of her ill-temper. She snapped at the assistant, hurried her on, then criticized the results of her work. When she went she left a small tip and a nasty atmosphere. She stuffed the newspapers deep in her bag, so that no one would think she had been concerning herself with anything as totally irrelevant as Bridget's reviews. She walked out into the sun again, moving her shoulders in an aggressive swagger. After a moment or two her mouth twisted into an unpleasant smile, as if she had thought of something brutal to say during rehearsal. She sweated.

She came to the Prince of Wales Theatre and pushed open the stage-door. Sergeant Harrison was not around. Usually Gaylene rather liked exchanging stentorian greetings and parade-ground insults with him, particularly during the recent series of test matches, when she had invariably had the trump card. But last night he had seen her leave the theatre. Perhaps it was just as well he was not there. She flicked through the mail in the stage-door-keeper's office, peered at the provenance of everyone else's, and took up one addressed to herself. Bound to be an offer. The smile seemed to anticipate that it would be one to make the rest green with envy. She drew her fleshy arms across her forehead.

'Bloody heat,' she said to Bob, assistant stage-door-keeper, as he came towards her and seemed to be about to protest that she was not allowed to go through the mail. 'It's worse than Australia, because here the cities are so bloody dirty. Look at my dress, will you? It's positively clinging to me!'

She thrust her body forward. Her dress was, indeed, positively clinging to her. That's some compensation, anyway, she seemed to say as she looked down at herself with superb self-satisfaction.

She didn't open the letter, but she started towards her dressing-room, clutching it, and covering it with sweaty marks. She marched purposefully through the dark, dusty passageways. Passing Calvin Cross she saluted him distantly. Passing

Owen Caulfield, looking busy and self-important on this, a big day for him, she greeted him more affectionately. Gaylene always had a soft spot for people she had slept with. She came to her dressing-room, did not notice the metal doormat in front of it, put down her bag, and clutching the letter in her left hand, put her right hand on the doorknob.

# CHAPTER VII

*Gendarmes' Duet*

Gaylene had been electrocuted. That much was certain.

The light-socket over the dressing-table near the door had been dismantled, and connected with a length of new wire to the old brass doorknob and to a metal doormat which had been placed outside the door. Gaylene, sweaty and scantily dressed, had stood on the doormat, placed her hand on the knob, and had thus made a perfect circuit.

That much, then was certain. Gaylene had died almost instantly, had not even had time to wonder which of her various chickens had come home to roost. That was left to the police.

Three hours after Gaylene's fleshy form had quivered for the last time, the situation in the Prince of Wales Theatre was a pattern of extreme contrasts—contrasts of activity in one part of the building with lethargy in another, memories of a life departed here, signs of life continuing there. Perhaps the oddest of the signs of life continuing was in the foyer, where queues had formed for future performances of the Northern Opera. Successful as they had been in attracting audiences, the box office had never known such a day. Even from the early hours, the reviews of Bridget's Fiordiligi the night before had stimulated an interest well beyond the normal, but the news of Gaylene's death—broadcast over the local radio stations and reported in the stop-press of the evening papers—aroused in Mancunians such a desire to patronize opera that two windows were now open for booking—one for *Così*, one for other performances, and the two ladies behind the windows were so busy parrying questions that they had no time to catch up on the latest developments themselves.

Calvin called the two queues that had formed the connoisseurs and the ghouls. He himself had been spotted by someone in the ghouls' queue—his skin made him instantly recognizable—and he had had to make a hasty and undignified retreat into the auditorium pursued by five or six Mancunian vultures, pretending to ask for his autograph but in fact only eager for carrion and quite careless of behavioural niceties in the acquisition of it.

'What a mob!' said Calvin, in the empty vastness of the stalls. Then he perceived a shadowy form, hunched in the middle of the auditorium, looking towards the stage. It was Owen, deep in thought, or perhaps orchestrating a rehearsal that was not in fact taking place. 'What a mob!' repeated Calvin, going towards him. 'They looked as if they'd like to have torn me limb from limb.'

Owen grunted, and then said: 'Leave me alone, will you, Calvin? I've got a lot to think about.'

Calvin left him without another word. Looking back from one of the side exits he saw he had resumed his pensive pose. He never understood Owen. Was he trying to say he was grief-stricken for Gaylene? And if so, was it true? No—it couldn't possibly be. It occurred to Calvin that Owen adopted poses, and that he did it not so much to impress other people as to bolster up himself *to* himself. But Calvin was not one to psychoanalyse his colleagues, and he put the thought from him.

Then something else occurred to him. Could Owen have some idea who had done it? Could he have seen something that gave it away—for example, in Gaylene's dressing-room?

For in point of fact, Owen had had a pretty nasty day. He had greeted Gaylene as he passed her in the corridor, and then, as he turned a corner into a passage leading to the stage, something had made him look back. Gaylene had been in a rigid, ludicrous position, as if glued to the doorknob. Owen had shouted for the assistant stage-door-keeper, and as they had watched, Gaylene had sunk slowly to the floor, very, very dead. Trying to pull her from the knob, Owen had had a minor shock, then he and Bob had raced together round to a small, dimly-lit passage which ran between the Prince of Wales and the neighbouring Woolworth's, and from there they had wriggled, pushed and squirmed their way through a dirty little window which was the only connection that the dressing-room had with the outside world. When, after a time, their eyes had managed to accustom themselves to the gloom, they had seen the little device of wires passing from the light-socket to the door. At that point, Owen had collapsed on a chair and had been very sick.

\* \* \*

Raymond Ricci had arrived from the airport barely half a minute after the police had gone in. He had found a little knot of company members outside the stage door, aimless and glum. They knew little beyond the obvious fact of the death, and they had been registering their impressions of the policemen who, if their suspicions were correct, seemed destined to be poking their noses into everybody's private business for the next few days or weeks.

'What's up?' called Raymond cheerily as he paid off his taxi. 'Are the brokers in?'

There was an awkward pause. Nobody has managed to coin a polite formula to cover the fact that someone has been murdered.

'It's Gaylene,' said Bridget finally.

'Christ!' said Raymond Ricci. 'What does that mean—hospital visiting with grapes? Fruit for the fruity?'

'It means she's dead,' said Simon Mulley flatly. Then, because that was what everyone was assuming, he added: 'Murdered.'

'Christ,' said Raymond Ricci again, looking genuinely shocked, though not particularly sorry. Then no one seemed to know what to say, and they just stood around a little longer in their aimless group.

'I suppose no one wants to hear about Oslo?' said Raymond Ricci at last.

But nobody did.


As soon as he got the call from the theatre Superintendent Nichols knew this was going to be one hell of a case. As he looked at the little device attached to the doorknob and doormat he felt that his instinct had been jusified. So simple; so silly, even. And yet, it had worked to perfection. The contributory factors that had made it so doubly lethal—the hot day, the fact that she was sweating profusely, all these were things the murderer could have, and probably had, counted on, and thus he had managed to bring about a quick, perfect kill.

The mere thought of the ramifications of this case made Nichols wilt. The various attempts previous to the successful one, for example: he had read about (and sniffed suspiciously over) these practice runs in the press, and the thought of checking up the various alibis of a whole opera company was the stuff of which policemen's nightmares are made. Then all the theatricality, the boasting, the attitudinizing that he would be letting himself in for—but he was getting in front of himself, and he pulled himself together. No point in taking your hurdles early. He turned to a passing constable, and said: 'We'll want the best shorthand writer in the force for this case. It's going to be one hell of a complicated one, if I'm not mistaken. If we can't have Chappell, I want nothing less than McLintock, and make that clear to them at Headquarters.'

After making a close survey of the dressing-room, Nichols left it to the experts, who could be relied on to find something to do there for hours yet. In the corridor he met up with Sergeant Chappell, bright, bushy tailed and a shorthand whizz-kid, and together they went looking for an office. They needed one if they were to be jawing and niggling at the various company members for days, as he suspected they would.

'The stage-door-keeper's away today,' said Nichols, and they went and looked at his little room. Bob was there, and he protested that Sergeant Harrison wouldn't like it, but he looked the type who was used to not getting his own way, and Nichols overruled him.

'I'm sure Sergeant Harrison will understand our needs,' he said. 'I like the look of this place. It smells military.'

And he immediately began settling himself in.

Superintendent Nichols was in his forties—stocky, not yet running to fat, and not yet worn down by his job into weariness or cynicism. Perhaps the close observer would notice something sad about his eyes, something withdrawn, as if he saw more than he wanted of things that had no cure. But on the surface Nichols was a cheerful, business-like man, who worried about his family, and did his job efficiently. He had no flamboyance, not an ounce of skill at public relations, and so he was a breed of top policemen that is dying out. His accent was not broad, but he was a Lancashire man through and through. He could keep his counsel as well as any man on the Manchester force.

Settled into the stage-door office, a roomy place that seemed to double with lost-property office and was neatly stored with old umbrellas, odd shoes, walking sticks and bags of all kinds, Nichols set about the task of getting the immediate facts square and ship-shape. He got on to Headquarters and had them look out all the newspaper cuttings on the previous attempts, as well as anything else they could dig up on Gaylene. Then he called in Mike Turner to start filling in his own mental picture of the girl whose hefty body was still prone in the corridors of the theatre, surrounded by all the official technicians of death.

His first impressions of Mike were none too favourable. Mancunians do not greatly like smooth people, especially smooth Mancunians. Nichols certainly distrusted people who dressed casually in a way that could only be described as impeccable. That sort of wear was for glossy ads. After a time, though, he began to detect a nervousness in Mike, which removed some of his distrust, and he wondered if it was a congenital personal nervousness. It was almost as if the smoothness was only a cover—but for what Nichols did not feel sure.

'I understand you're what we might call the boss of the company, is that right, sir?' said Nichols in his not-too-bright-policeman manner.

'In a way, I suppose, Superintendent,' said Mike, smiling brilliantly, and then switching the smile off suddenly when he realized exactly why he was being interviewed. 'I'm the administrator, or director—call it what you will. And I'm chief conductor as well. Normally these would be two quite distinct posts, of course, but we're a small company, with a very small subsidy, and of course we have to cut our suit according to our cloth.'

'In any case, it would be you who engaged Miss Ffrench as a member of the company?'

'That's right. I saw her Carmen at Cardiff. There were all sorts of things wrong with the performance, but still it did have a lot of life . . . guts—

call it what you will. My idea was that she'd go down well here in some of the earthier parts.'

'So she'd only been in Manchester since the beginning of the present season?' asked Nichols.

'That's right. *Rigoletto*—that's the piece we should be rehearsing now—would have been her first opera with us, and it had a very good role for her.'

'So she'd been around for a few weeks, had she?'

'That's right.'

'How had she fitted in with the rest of the company?'

'Oh, very well. She was a . . . frank, open kind of girl . . . everyone liked her very . . . Do you want the truth?'

'Yes.'

'Everyone thought she was a pain in the neck.'

Mike Turner settled back in his chair, and smiled his handsome, charming smile, as if it was a great relief to him to have told the truth. Nichols's eyes narrowed infinitesimally. Turner reminded him of a certain brand of politician.

'Well, thank you for being honest about that,' said Nichols, 'though I imagine we would probably have got the idea before too long. Could you tell me why she wasn't liked?'

'I can't speak for the others,' said Turner cautiously. 'You'd better ask them. But for myself alone, I'd say that she was as vulgar, boastful, and untruthful as anyone I've ever met, and one of the biggest trollops to boot.'

The somewhat old-fashioned language slipped elegantly off Mike's tongue. Again he leaned back in his chair, and smiled his charming-adolescent smile.

'She slept around, I take it,' murmured Nichols.

'She slept around,' assented Mike.

'With you, sir?'

'A couple of times, when she first got here—no, three. I suspect she decided to start at the top and work her way down.'

'She went on elsewhere, then. Who to, do you know?'

'Owen Caulfield, in the first place, I think. And then Raymond Ricci, and then—God knows who. You'd better ask one of the women—they probably kept their eyes on her.'

'Why did you split up, sir?'

'Split up? I don't know that we split up, not as I understand the term. You can only split up if you've been going together, can't you? We just went to bed a couple of times, then didn't go to bed. I think that was pretty much the pattern with Gaylene.'

'You would say she was something of a nymphomaniac?'

'I'd say she was a nymphomaniac.'

'If she went to bed with so many, I presume not all the company can have thought her a pain in the neck?'

'I don't think that follows, Superintendent. People went to bed with her *and* thought her a pain in the neck. It happens all the time, you know.'

Nichols sighed, and went on. 'These attacks on her—'

'You'd better ask Owen Caulfield about those, or

someone who was at the rehearsals. This was to be the first orchestral rehearsal today, so I haven't really been in on things. All I know is, no one's been taking them terribly seriously. Rather typically Gaylene, they were, so everyone thought.'

'Until today.'

'Right. Right.' Mike looked obviously nervous and uncertain for the first time in the interview, and then repeated: 'Right. Of course everyone will be having second thoughts now. And in point of fact, when she made the first accusation, I know everybody thought she did a pretty convincing acting job.'

'These attempts, or supposed attempts, complicate things for us,' said Nichols. 'I was wondering if you could help me there. If you were to ask your whole company to write down—on a card, say—what they were doing at the relevant times, that would save an awful lot of routine questioning.'

'I could, of course,' said Mike dubiously. 'But two-thirds of the company would never even have swapped words with Gaylene—members of the orchestra, the chorus, the stage-hands, and so on. Do you think it would be worth it?'

'I think it would, sir. For one thing it makes it less invidious. Of course we'll be checking up mainly on those who seem to come into the picture as possible suspects, but at least in the first instance I'd like to make our enquiries as general as possible. I'll give you the dates and times as soon as I've got the newspaper reports from HQ. Then perhaps you could talk to the whole company together.'

'Very well. Anything to help.' Mike seemed a

little embarrassed. 'By the way, this probably seems heartless, but I was wondering when we could start using the theatre again—for rehearsals and so on.'

'Well, I hope tomorrow,' said Nichols. 'I imagine we can finish with the stage and auditorium then, since there's not likely to be much of interest there. But there'll be a lot of restrictions on the back-stage areas—tomorrow and for some days to come, I imagine.'

'We can get around that,' said Mike, already planning the rehearsal for tomorrow and a show-must-go-on speech.

'Of course,' said Nichols, 'as far as we are concerned the crucial time is that for the present attempt, the successful one. I imagine it could have been set up at any time from last night onwards, and we'll want to know who had access to the dressing-room, and so on. Who would you suggest I see?'

'Well—Sergeant Harrison, of course. The stage-door-keeper. Knows everything about the theatre there is to know—and pretty much the same about most of the members of the company. Actually he's off sick today. Bloody lucky for him as it turns out: he usually goes round checking the rooms in the morning before a rehearsal. But he was on last night, so he may have gone round checking up after the performance was over.'

'About what time would that be, sir?'

'Fairly late. There was an awful lot of cheering for Miss Lander—very exciting. The last of the audience wouldn't have left until about a quarter to eleven. Then of course the cast would have been mulling around a bit afterwards—there's always a lot of fuss and congratulations after an evening of that kind. I'd been back-stage, but I went off afterwards with one of the local businessmen: trying to persuade him to sponsor a new production specially for Miss Lander. She came along later. I would imagine the whole cast was here till a quarter or half past eleven, at the very least.'

'Well, we'll get on to Harrison as soon as we can. Now, I'll probably want to see you again later, sir, but before you go, is there anything about the girl herself, her relationships with the others and so on that you think we ought to know? I just ask because you could save us a lot of time.'

For the first time in the interview Superintendent Nichols almost liked Mike Turner. His cool manner, his air of sitting for his own portrait to a fashionable photographer, were all forgotten, and he seemed to be wrestling with himself as to whether to say anything or not. Finally he muttered: 'I'd rather you asked Owen Caulfield that. As I say, he's been in on all the rehearsals. And it is my company, you see—'

As he went out, Superintendent Nichols turned to Sergeant Chappell, the shorthand genius, and raised an interrogative eyebrow.

'That's the sort of chap that makes people want to abolish Manchester Grammar,' said Chappell curtly.

'Watch it,' said Nichols. 'You're talking to an old boy.'

*　*　*

There was no prospect of rehearsal that day. It was early evening by the time Mike Turner called the company together in the stalls and told them that there would be a regular *Rigoletto* rehearsal the next day, possibly without many back-stage facilities. He went on to report to them Superintendent Nichols's request concerning alibis for the various attempts on Gaylene's life. He tried to avoid using the word alibis, but for the life of him he could think of no other. Then he exhorted them to help the police as far as possible, and come to the memorial service when it was arranged. Then they all drifted off, leaving their addresses with the constable on the door.

It was a strange end to a strange day. For Owen it was not quite ended, since he had been asked to go along to see Nichols in the stage-door office. The others, uncertain of what was to come, and not even quite sure what had actually happened, did not know what they ought to feel. What they actually did feel was an odd mixture of fear, excitement, pity and apprehension—a sort of catharsis. Nobody felt any grief for Gaylene, and nobody had the bad taste to pretend to feel any.

In the course of the evening, though, various obituaries were said over her. The *Guardian* had had its ready, and altered it slightly to suit the circumstances of her death. After a summary of her brief career to date (rather less spectacular than it had always sounded in Gaylene's own version) it said that her death was 'a tragically early end to a career of exceptional premise'. They probably meant 'promise'.

In Calvin's pokey rooms not far from the Methodist Hall, he and Bridget brewed Nescafé, talked over last night's *Così*, and inevitably went on from that to the murder.

'Well,' said Calvin, who like most of the rest of the cast could not find it in him to be nicer to Gaylene in death than he had been to her in raucous, flabby life, 'this is one murder you don't have to look for a motive for. It was Gaylene—that was motive enough.'

But in the pub in the west of the city, where it had been rumoured, wrongly, that bottles of Resch's lager were to be had, Hurtle, relaxing after a game, grew almost lachrymose over a pint of English imitation beer, as he called it, and quite embarrassed the team-mates with him by coming close to showing a strong emotion: 'She was a marvellous lay, but not for someone in training,' he said, gazing introspectively into the flat brown depths of his pint mug.

# CHAPTER VIII

*Producer*

It was nearly nine in the evening when Nichols went over with Owen Caulfield the last moments of Gaylene Ffrench, and the finding of the little wire trick that·cut off her career of exceptional promise. Owen had looked around him uncertainly as he had come in to Sergeant Harrison's orderly little office with the neat piles of other people's belongings and the lines of nails with keys on them. He sprawled himself somewhat diffidently in the armchair, and then tried to sit up straight, as if this were some kind of confirmation class. Nichols was by now fairly used to people who did not quite know how to behave when confronted with the death of an obvious monster like Gaylene, but Owen from the first struck him as a puzzling and rather unnerving character. He could add nothing to what the police already knew about the death of Gaylene except a fairly exact time—between five and ten past twelve. He also gave them a gruff description of the process of her dying.

In a sense, what he added of most value to Nichols's knowledge of the affair was himself. Nichols sat at Sergeant Harrison's little desk, form-

ing the sort of instant impressions that are a policeman's business, categorizing and cross-referencing
in his mind, and one of the first things he registered was that Owen was not at all interested in
doing the same thing to him. In Nichols's experience this was very rare in people being interviewed about any serious matter: whether they
were suspect or witness, innocent or guilty, almost
all looked closely at their interrogator, tried to
sum him up, see where he could be appealed to,
what were his weak points.

Owen made no attempt at all to do any of these
things. It could have been because he was so
upset, though he did not now look upset; it could
have been because he was so completely innocent
that the thought did not occur to him, but Nichols
wanted to reserve judgement about his innocence
or guilt; in fact he suspected the reason to be that
Owen was one of those people for whom other
people are never more than objects, to be used,
bullied, cajoled—though usually ineffectually, because they are not understood. Put in a situation
where he had no authority, Owen was out at sea,
and searching for a new identity, a new attitude.
Basically, it seemed to Nichols that he was a very
empty person, and that he was panicked by his
emptiness.

Owen made no bones about the fact that he
had slept with Gaylene. Mike had already told him
the Superintendent knew this.

'Yes, we went together for a bit, not very long
after she arrived,' he said, as if it was a matter of
no importance.

'For how long?' asked Nichols.

'About a week or so, as far as I remember,' said Owen. 'Certainly not more than ten days.'

'Who broke things off?'

'I don't know that anyone did,' said Owen. 'I started rehearsing the *Rigoletto* production, and the whole thing just sort of faded out—you know how it is.'

She broke it off, said Nichols to himself. He said: 'And she went on to Raymond Ricci, a member of the cast, is that right?'

'I think so. Among others.'

'You weren't jealous?'

'Good Lord no. There's always someone like Gaylene in any theatre company, Superintendent. Sleeps around with most of the actors, moves from one to another in a matter of days. People just sleep with her as a matter of convenience—one never gets actually involved with someone like that.'

Owen's manner was man-of-the-world. Nichols was watching him closely, but try as he might he couldn't penetrate the pose to find out his actual attitude to his affair with Gaylene.

'I gather on the whole that Miss Ffrench was not generally liked, is that right?' Nichols said.

'I suppose not,' said Owen judiciously. 'She didn't go out of her way to be, certainly. On the other hand, I doubt whether you could say she was positively *dis*liked. If you were sensible you didn't take her seriously enough to dislike her.'

'Who would you say got on least well with her?' Nichols asked.

There was a pause, and Nichols could feel Owen changing his pose from one of judicial impartiality to one of an agonized wrestler with his conscience. Nichols was beginning to find these roles the most fascinating thing about Owen. He guessed that in a situation where his authority as producer meant nothing, Owen had had to give up his usual performance and was desperately thrashing around to find another. The poses were all of lay figures, and Nichols wondered whether Owen even convinced himself.

'Well,' Owen said finally, 'I suppose you could say it was Calvin Cross.' All at once there came into Owen's voice the strident bleat of the congenital agitator, the collector of grievances. 'You're not to jump to any conclusions, though. Calvin is black, but the sort of prejudice one meets all the time in officialdom simply isn't going to do much longer. Calvin was born in this country, and he's as British as you or I. The police are going to have to change their attitude to the coloured community, with a new generation growing up, and people like Calvin among them.'

It was quite the most unconvincing of the poses Owen had adopted thus far. By the end he was beginning to sound lame even to himself. Nichols could only assume that it was adopted on the spur of the moment to somehow compensate for having mentioned Calvin's name at all. He allowed himself the luxury of a pause, and then said:

'In my experience the police give the benefit of the doubt to the coloured community rather more often than the general public gives it to the police. But let's not get side-tracked. I'm interested in Calvin Cross not because he's coloured, but because you say he disliked—'

'Not disliked. I didn't use that word.'

'—because he didn't get on too well, then, with Gaylene Ffrench. I presume from what you've just been saying that Miss Ffrench made some remarks about him being coloured, is that right?'

'Yes, that's so. He and Bridget Lander got engaged, and she seemed outraged at the idea.'

'That's rather odd, isn't it?'

'She was Australian, remember,' said Owen.

'My experience of young Australians doesn't suggest they are that far behind the world on questions of that sort,' said Nichols.

'Gaylene was not exactly an average Australian,' said Owen.

'Ah . . . But I thought you were suggesting just now that she was. I wonder, now, if there might not have been something else behind it than pure old-fashioned colour-prejudice.'

'Well, I don't know,' said Owen, resuming his agonized-conscience pose. 'Most of the trouble between them came because she was trying to give a super-sexy performance, a Sadie Thompson job, and he wasn't responding in any way.'

'So there was an element of the personal in their relationship. I gather Mr Cross was probably not one of the ones who went to bed with Miss Ffrench.'

'I believe not,' said Owen. 'So far as I know.' Then he added: 'I suppose that was basically the trouble.'

'She was playing for him and didn't get him?'

'Yes. She was playing as only she knew how. But Calvin wasn't at all attracted.'

From what he had heard thus far of Gaylene,

Nichols was only surprised that anyone ever was.

'I presume she gave up after Mr Cross got engaged?'

'In a way. She'd rather lost hope by then anyway. But she kept on nagging at him in a way that I know got under Bridget's skin.'

'They had words, did they?'

'Yes, they had words.'

'If Miss Ffrench didn't sleep with Mr Cross, who else did she sleep with?'

Owen considered, and then spread out his hands in a would-be-Italianate gesture.

'Who knows? How deep is the ocean? But the ones I know are Mike Turner, myself, Raymond Ricci—we mentioned him, he's a bass, Anglo-Italian family, rather handsome—and then James McKaid—Northern Irishman, chip-on-the-shoulder type, not generally liked in the company. Oh yes, and then of course her Australian boy-friend when he got here, just a few days ago.'

'Yes,' said Nichols, 'I have a picture of him here. Rugby player.' Nichols gazed at the bottomless good-humour of Hurtle's smile, beaming out from that morning's paper. 'I suppose all the sleeping around stopped when he arrived?'

'Oh yes, I imagine so. Yes, he and she have been around together since then, I think. She missed a rehearsal Wednesday to cheer him on at the game, she said.'

'So he wouldn't know about all the others?'

'That I couldn't say.'

'You don't think he could have been jealous?'

There was a long pause.

'Certainly he didn't show it,' said Owen finally.

It occurred to Nichols that Owen was contriving to cast doubt on, or emphatically not to remove doubt from, an extremely large number of people. He had noticed the insistence on 'Anglo-Italian', so unexpected from one who had just proclaimed Calvin's Britishness. He had noticed the emphasis on McKaid's chip on the shoulder. It seemed a particularly odd attitude for a producer to take up about members of his own cast.

'What had your own relations been with Miss Ffrench since you—stopped going together?' Nichols asked.

'Oh, perfectly amicable. She was a good rehearser. We just had a normal professional relationship.'

'There were no artistic disagreements, shall we call them? About how the part should be played, or that sort of thing?'

'None at all. It's a quite simple and straightforward part, hers. If you give it plenty of sex it comes out all right. Gaylene did this, and that was fine by me.'

'I see,' said Nichols. 'It struck me she might have had ideas of her own, and not be easy to produce.'

'All opera-singers have ideas of their own,' said Owen sourly. 'Not very good ones either, as a rule.' Then he removed the sneer from his lips and said with affected tolerance: 'Of course one has to work these things out at rehearsal. It's all a matter of give and take, you know.'

Nichols thought that if it was advice and criticism that was being talked about, he had seldom seen anyone more likely to give and less likely to take it. He led Owen on to giving an account of the first attempt on Gaylene's life, as reported by Gaylene herself. Owen stressed how convincing she had been initially, and how scepticism had only set in later. Of the other attempt, he only knew what he had read in the papers. As he was preparing to leave, the interview at an end, Nichols said casually: 'Oh, by the way, where were you last night?'

Owen jumped, as if stung, and opened his mouth as if to shout a reply. Almost immediately he remembered where he was and who he was talking to.

'Well,' he said, 'I was at home early on, then I came to the theatre to see how *Così Fan Tutte* was doing. It was Miss Lander's first performance with the company, you see, and I'd rehearsed the production last season. Then I went back-stage to congratulate her, and there was a bit of a crowd, so pretty soon I went home.'

'I see,' said Nichols. 'Well, I think that's all you can help us with at the moment, sir.'

It had been an odd reaction, he thought, as Owen closed the door behind him. Almost automatic, as if he was quite unable to let anybody question, criticize or go against him. He felt—as, being a policeman, he often had felt—how dangerous a little authority was. It was the easiest of all drugs to get hooked on. Or had the reaction meant more than that? He looked at Sergeant Chappell, who once again had on his eager young face an expression of distaste.

'What did you make of him?' asked Nichols.

'The age of team-spirit is dead,' said Chappell.

'Hadn't you registered that till now?' said Nich-

ols. 'It's only in the force we cover up for our
mates. What sort of general impression did he
make on you?'

'Rather a nasty individual, if you ask me,' said
Chappell. 'Nasty temper.'

'True. This is one murder, though, that certainly
doesn't have the look of having been done in a fit
of temper.'

'Very unsure of himself too,' went on Chappell.
'Puts on a series of poses the whole time, depending on what's being asked. You never once got a
sincere reaction out of him.'

'That's what I noticed most. Seems to me the
sort of chap who's always trying to impose himself on people, or to impress them in one way or
another. And when he's in a situation where that
isn't possible, he quite simply doesn't know what
to do.'

'Interesting to hear what the cast will have to
say about *him*,' said Chappell. 'I'd bet the atmosphere has been less than happy-families during
the rehearsals.'

'Yes, I'm looking forward to hearing that. And
then there's this Sergeant Harrison. According to
Turner he knows practically all there is to know
about this mob. I'd have him in tonight if he was
around, but as he's sick we'd better give him till
tomorrow. The technical boys will have reported
by then, so he'll probably be able to help us on
that side as well.'

But the words were hardly out of his mouth
when the telephone rang. He picked up the phone.

'Is that t'lad in charge of this 'ere murder case?'
said the voice at the other end.

'That's right. Nichols is the name.'

'Aye, well this is 'Arrison. Stage-door-keeper. Sergeant 'Arrison they call me.'

'Your name was just on our lips,' said Nichols. 'We'd like to talk to you.'

'Not 'alf so mooch as I want to talk to you,' said Sergeant Harrison. 'I'd've been down before, but I've only just realized.'

'Can we come and see you, perhaps?'

'No need. I've just had a spot of my old trouble. Malaria—it comes back now and then. Relic of Malaya, that is. Nothing serious. You'll be pretty busy at t'theatre, I reckon, and I'm right as rain now, so I'll be on my way in two ticks to see you. I could kick myself for not having thought of it sooner.'

'We could send a car for you.'

'No need. I'm not a bloody invalid, man.'

And Sergeant Harrison rang off. There was someone who was blunt, direct and to-the-point, thought Nichols. He was going to be a nice change after these theatre people.

Sergeant Harrison knocked out his pipe in the ash-tray on the mantelpiece, and looked with affection at the framed photograph of his daughter in Bir-mingham standing just beside it. She's what I'd call a fine figure of a girl, he said to himself with a sort of self-satisfaction. Not like these willowy creatures you see around these days. Then he looked at the mirror, and began tying a dark blue tie with military precision over a light blue shirt. Then he took out a pair of hair-brushes, and pun-ished his hair into the sort of rigid, disciplined style that one used to see in hair-cream advertisements thirty or forty years ago. The police were men with standards themselves, he thought, looking at the result. They were going to be interested in what he had to tell them. And they couldn't know too soon.

Then Sergeant Harrison went into the hall and cast an appraising eye over the coat-rack. The day had been hot, but it could be chilly at this time of night. Best not to take chances in the circumstances, not after the malaria bout. He'd need to be at the theatre tomorrow—to see all the fuss and excitement, and keep a bit of order about the place. He took down a navy blue rain-coat, rather naval in style, and belted it around his substantial frame. Then, with a last look in the hall mirror to see that he was presentable, the pardonable vanity of a military man, he checked in his pocket that he had the key, and opened the front door.

As he stepped out into the near-darkness he uttered first a sharp grunt of surprise, then a louder grunt as he felt the long, thin knife enter through his ribs. His body went rigid with pain, and as he toppled forward the abundant life left him in a long emission that was halfway between a breath and a shout. It ended in an undignified gurgle.

Thus died Sergeant Harrison of the Prince of Wales Theatre, formerly of the Royal Artillery, whose ancestors had fought for their Sovereign as soldiers of the line at Agincourt, Malplaquet and Waterloo, and for their class at Peterloo and factory gates throughout the grimier parts of the North of England. Their graves were unmarked lumps of foreign soil, or off-white tombstones of inferior stone and knobbly design. Sergeant Harrison's own immediate destination was the police morgue, where he lay side by side with Gaylene Ffrench, both fine figures, and a tribute to the care and feeding of their respective countries.

Next morning Mike Turner asked his company to add another date and time to the little alibi cards they were writing for Superintendent Nichols.

# CHAPTER IX

*Lower Registers*

It was a sad and tired Superintendent Nichols who got back to the Prince of Wales Theatre next day a little after twelve. He had been up half the night, attending the last police rites over the body of Sergeant Harrison, and these had been difficult and depressing. Peering with the aid of police lamps at the body of a man not long past his prime, questioning the neighbours, going through the orderly little house, and hearing the howls of his dog—this was the sort of thing he ought to be used to and case-hardened by, but he was not. His sleep had been short and fitful, and by morning his mind had become possessed of the conviction that the murderer he was after was of a quick and daring mind and utterly ruthless by temperament. The murder of Gaylene Ffrench was one thing: though obviously premeditated, it was clear that the girl had made herself so effortlessly objectionable to everyone within range of insult that, in so far as murder is ever understandable to a normal, gentle person, hers could well be. But the immediate follow-up, simply to gain self-protection, this suggested quite something else: someone cruel and quite beyond the normal operations of the human conscience. This was a murderer who had to be caught and caught quickly.

Almost as soon as he arrived at the theatre Nichols saw for the first time someone who by all ordinary standards ought to be considered a prime suspect for the murders. If anyone stood to gain by Gaylene's death (beyond, that is, the general gain of not having her around any longer) that person was her understudy. And in the darkened theatre, in the hour before the general rehearsal began, Nichols saw Calvin Cross and Mr Pettifer helping her to prepare for her big chance.

Barbara Bootle was, like Gaylene, a big girl. Hefty was the word her relations used, and she wished they wouldn't. She was a tall, heavy Lancashire girl, without an atom of sex, and nothing but an ever-ready blush and a shame-faced manner to suggest that the subject had ever been brought to her attention. Lost among the other boys and girls of the chorus, she had done what everyone else had done and had been Sicilian peasant women or medieval German maiden without attracting attention to herself. Her rich, edgy mezzo had won her promotion to understudy Gaylene, and she had prayed every night that Gaylene (who had effortlessly ignored her existence) would remain in the blooming good health which seemed her birthright. 'Any other part, Lord,' she said in her rich Lancashire brogue, 'but not a whore.' And now the part was hers, not just for one or two, but for all performances.

She stood on the stage, her shoulders sagging, her face crimson, contemplating a point on the floor with rapt attention. There was an angularity about her body that suggested she had had to be corsetted in iron to keep her limbs together, and that otherwise she would be sprawled limply on the stage like a puppet whose master has let go of the strings. She seemed to be praying to her God to advance Armageddon to some date before the first performance.

'If you'll just let me put my arm around your waist,' Calvin said tentatively. 'That's all that's necessary, really.'

Miss Bootle nodded miserably, and her shoulders straightened to a military rigidity. When Calvin's black hand appeared around her other side her eyes fixed themselves on the middle distance and her mouth set itself in a firm line, like an early Christian martyr waiting for her turn with the lion.

'If you could just relax a little,' said Calvin, 'laugh . . . roll your eyes . . .' She looked at him in panic. 'Well, perhaps that's not necessary, but if you could just loosen up a bit and try to *enjoy* it.'

Barbara Bootle bared her teeth in a dreadful smile.

'Like this?' she said.

Even from the middle of the stalls Nichols could see she was shaking all over. On the whole, she seemed a very poor starter as a suspect. The knife that went through Sergeant Harrison's ribs was surely propelled on its way by sterner nerves than these.

When Nichols talked to Raymond Ricci it was mid-afternoon, and he had just finished his Act i, scene ii appearance in the first full rehearsal of

*Rigoletto.* Nichols had stood in the darkened theatre, and had seen him show his menacing, thinbladed sword to Rigoletto: 'You see before you a man who bears a sword.' Memories of the wound in Sergeant Harrison's side as he lay in his own little front garden in the spot-lights rigged up by the police flooded through Nichols's mind, and reality and performance seemed for one moment to merge and be one. It had been an unnerving experience.

Now Ricci sat before him, his sallowness increased by bold make-up, his legs clad in black tights, his upper half in what on stage looked like a rough coat of animal skin, though close up it looked and smelt more of the plastics factory than of any beast in creation.

Raymond was still tensed up after his big scene: though off-stage he exuded generally a sort of Mediterranean languor, the stage always set his nerves tingling, and today was the first time he had sung his role with the orchestra. Perhaps that was why he was so unusually on edge, making nervous little gestures with his hands, and now and then screwing up his eyes compulsively.

'Yes, we went together for a bit,' he said, throwing out his right arm in a gesture of frankness. 'I suppose you'll have heard that from someone by now, knowing the people around here. We went together. Not for long, though.'

'How long, sir?'

'Just as long as I could stand her. If I remember rightly, that was a little over a week.'

'You slept together, but you didn't actually like

her, is that right?' said Nichols, feeling horribly square.

'That's about it,' said Ricci, blinking. 'She wasn't likeable, as I'm sure you've gathered by now, not likeable at all. But she was available. And how.'

'Certainly the impression I've got,' said Nichols, 'is that Miss Ffrench was, shall we say, decidedly cooperative.'

'She'd sleep with anyone who asked her and a good many who didn't,' said Raymond, smiling briefly and not too attractively. 'Not that I'm suggesting I was reluctant, or anything. Still, she went through men like other women go through paper tissues. She kept me on longer than most—two or three nights was par for the course, I believe. Actually, it was me who gave her the push, not *vice versa*.'

'Why, sir?'

'Well, as you can guess, I suppose, she became a bore.' He leaned forward in his chair to get his point over to Nichols. 'She was very enjoyable for a few nights—she'd been well-trained at Coonabarrabran High, I'll give her that—but along with her you had to take that thundering, blundering, bull-dozing egotism, that was the rub. Of course we're all egotists in this game, more or less, but we all put up pretences—of sympathy, interest, pleasure in other people's successes, and so on. And how right we are. Because naked egotism like Gaylene's becomes the most crushing bore imaginable.'

During this long speech Raymond Ricci had become conscious of the jerky twistings of his hands, and he put them down heavily on the arm of the chair, and then reached into his pocket for his packet of cigarettes. Nichols watched him, wondering whether to believe that it had indeed been he who had broken off the affair (if that was the right word for so unromantic an arrangement) with Gaylene Ffrench.

'How did you end the . . . relationship, sir?' he asked. 'Were there rows, scenes, that sort of thing?'

'Good Lord no. 'Fraid not, Superintendent. I just said I wouldn't be coming round that night, and she said "Balls to you" or words to that effect. No, I lie: she actually said: "Balls to you." Then she made other arrangements, as she was bound to.'

'With Mr McKaid.'

'So I gathered later. And the best of luck to both of them.'

'You don't like him.'

'I didn't say that. But I would imagine that he and Gaylene would be pretty ideally suited to each other.'

'Tell me, what was your first reaction when Miss Ffrench made the accusation that someone was trying to kill her?'

'Well, it certainly wasn't surprise,' said Raymond Ricci, puffing at his cigarette thoughtfully. 'Oddly enough, I believed it, right from the beginning. I think like most I was impressed by the way she played it: she looked such a sight—all red and blotchy and vicious. But when she made so much mileage in publicity out of it, of course I had second thoughts and assumed it was just one of her little tricks. All of us did, I imagine, since we knew Gaylene.'

'She liked publicity?'

'She drank it up. She needed it like she needed T-bone steaks and peanut butter sandwiches. As far as I thought about it at all, I assumed that she resented all the stuff about Bridget and Calvin—'

'Their engagement?'

'That's right. The papers made quite a thing of it. I imagine she must have been green with envy, particularly as she hadn't managed to drag him into her unselective arms. So that's what made me change my mind and see it as a silly stunt.'

'But not now?'

'Well, obviously, one has to revise one's opinions—in the circumstances.'

Nichols watched him. An odd customer, he thought. By no means easy to know where you were with him, nor whether he was telling the truth. He was obviously relaxing now, presumably as the stimulus of the rehearsal was working off. The hands came to rest more often, and he was slipping down in his chair into a more comfortable position. But he was still not an easy person to come to terms with.

'Was there any connection that you know of between Miss Ffrench and Sergeant Harrison?'

'Connection? They joshed each other a lot— about the test matches, and that sort of thing— heavyweight fun, you know.' His face suddenly went serious. 'But I'm sorry about Harrison, we all are. It's a really dirty business. I didn't know him well, and he sometimes got on the wrong side of us, but he was a good chap. It's not like with Gaylene—no one could say that he asked for it.'

'You'd never talked to Harrison about Miss Ffrench, had you? He never told you anything— for example, anything that he'd noticed, about her private life, perhaps?'

'I'm afraid not, Superintendent. We only swopped the time of day. He wasn't really the kind of chap you had conversation with, unless you had some interest in common, like cricket, or the army. He kept his own counsel—you know the type.'

Nichols sighed. 'That's what I was rather afraid of,' he said.

'Now Gaylene was a different kettle of fish entirely,' said Ricci, becoming expansive. 'If she knew anything about anybody she'd tell it. Trouble was, you never knew what was true and what was dreamed up in her nasty little mind. Mostly one worked on the assumption that it was all a load of bull.'

'While you were . . . together, did she tell you anything that might suggest some sort of motive?' asked Nichols, walking down the path Ricci had rather obviously opened up for him. 'I mean, some motive beyond the general one of—'

'Of Gaylene being a pain in everybody's arse?'

'Yes, It *is* a motive, but not too good a one.'

'No, I suppose not. Except that we *are* theatricals, and that does make a difference. Well, let's see. Remembering her conversation is a bit like splashing round in a sewer. About Calvin, of course, she said the obvious—cold-fish, repressed homosexual, all that crap. "So much for the myth of the virility of blacks," she used to say. Actually, she said it to his face.'

'How did he react?'

'Very well. He just said: "So much for the myth of Anglo-Saxon reticence and self-control." I don't think she understood, though. Probably wasn't aware of being Anglo-Saxon. But it was a good reply. Luckily with Gaylene one could get a pretty good idea of the sort of thing she was likely to say, and think up something in advance.'

'What about the others?'

'Owen she was fairly careful with—he was letting her have her head, in the sense of letting her be as blatant and vulgar on stage as she could have wished, and so she went easy, in so far as was in her to. Bridget she riled the whole time, and Gaylene used to go on about how she would sing herself out in a couple of years' time—ruin the voice, you know. Usual professional spite. Simon Mulley —oh yes, she'd somehow got the idea he was a bigamist. She went on about it one night when we were in bed.'

'A bigamist?'

'Yes, God knows where she got that from. Used to lick her lips and say he must be a sex-maniac, which was pretty rich coming from her.'

'Didn't that make her interested in him?'

'Yes, of course. But she never got anywhere with him. If you *were* a bigamist you'd think twice about taking on Gaylene as well, I imagine. I think she decided it must have been a long time ago, and that he was past it now.'

'Anyone else?'

'Well, even Gaylene hadn't managed to dig up

anything on Mr Pettifer—that's the repetiteur. And
she hadn't had time to get anything on Giulia Contini. Jim McKaid she kept joshing about being a
member of the IRA, and though he told her over
and over again that he was a Protestant, she just
said "Same thing". God knows what she thought
she meant. She was abysmally ignorant about anything outside her own little circle of interest—
outside herself, that is.'

'And you, sir?'

'Oh, I was a pommie-wop. And probably a lot
more things when she was talking to someone else.
I think that about covers most of us, doesn't it?
One or two of the minor singers she hardly came
in contact with, since she only appears in the last
scene.'

'And Mr Turner?'

'Mike? Oh, the comparatively gentle treatment,
as with Owen. As far as that was possible with
Gaylene, you understand. Both of them were people she could hope to get something out of, in the
way of parts, or prominence, and so on. She was
no fool, and she knew which side her bread was
buttered. I think she was trying to get Mike to
put on *Samson and Delilah* or one of the other big
mezzo vehicles for her. But he's no fool either—I
doubt if he was responding.'

'You don't think she could have done the part?'

'Samson, yes. Delilah, hardly. But seriously, Gaylene wasn't that big a fish, and as far as Mike was
concerned she'd have to prove her drawing power
first. Anyway, we haven't the money for things a
bit outside the basic repertoire.'

'You yourself missed the second attempt on her, didn't you?' asked Nichols.

'That's right. I've just been catching up with it in the newspapers. Most of them don't have a great deal on it—I don't imagine they were taking her very seriously by then.'

'So you were away when the booby trap was set?'

Ricci stubbed out his cigarette. 'If it was set on Wednesday night or Thursday morning as everyone seems to be saying. I was in Oslo. She was dead when I got back.'

'We'll check that, of course, sir, but I imagine that means you're in the clear.'

'I've got the reviews,' said Ricci, reaching in his pocket. 'The chap who drove me to the station got me the morning papers. As I say, we singers are avid for publicity and reviews, even when we don't understand a word of them.'

The reviews were quite short. One of them said:

*Den Norske Opera bød igår på en meget lovende debut av Raymond Ricci fra Storbritannia. Han hadde en varm, følsom stemme, og det var noe sydlandsk over hans tolkningsmåte. Det var stor applaus. Vokalt følger hans Giovanni i Brownlee og Gobbi tradisjonen heller enn i Pinza og Siepi tradisjonen. Riccis utførelse lover godt for fremtiden, og med mer erfaring vil han bli blant dem man vil huska i rollen.*

Other reviews included such words as 'sukses', 'populære' and 'applaudert'. It seemed as if Ricci had gone down fairly big with the Oslo public.

'It's not a wonderful company,' said Ricci, with dubiously sincere self-depreciation. 'Rather provincial. One or two good voices, and some really rather dreadful ones. It's not exactly the big time.'

'The main thing is, it gives you an alibi,' said Nichols, not too interested in the operatic league division table. 'We'll check at the Oslo end, as I say, but it seems fairly clear. Well, I think that will be all. I'll let you get back to rehearsal.'

Raymond lit another cigarette as he got outside, and strolled back towards the stage. That hadn't been too bad, after all. As he neared the auditorium he heard Rigoletto and Gilda letting off every vocal firework in their armoury for the big duet at the end of Act II—he swearing vengeance on the Duke, she begging him to pardon her seducer. Giulia Contini's words being what they were, this last point hardly got across, but the impetus of the music carried the point fiercely through to the audience, though that audience was only Owen, Mr Pettifer, Calvin and one or two others. Raymond drew his hand across his forehead. It struck him, almost for the first time, that the emotions of opera were often rather remote from those of modern everyday life.


'Rather a smarmy individual,' said Sergeant Chappell.

'Let's have none of these racial smears,' said Nichols. 'Or you'll have nice Mr Caulfield on to us.'

'You can be smarmy and English,' said Sergeant Chappell. 'That one looked a typical womanizer to me.'

'That's not a term of abuse these days,' said Nichols. 'I agree he's probably a go-getter, with his eye on the main chance. On the other hand, he virtually admitted as much himself.'

'How far would you trust his reports about Gaylene Ffrench's conversation?'

Nichols shrugged. 'If he is entirely in the clear—and we'll have to check plane times and so on as well—he seems to have nothing to gain by lying. He reported it all pretty enthusiastically, I agree there. But it was mostly garbage, I imagine—it didn't seem to open up an obvious road to the truth. Pity he's in the clear, though. I could fancy him with a knife.'

'So could I. But he's not the only one in this company,' said Sergeant Chappell, with an expression of distaste. 'Who's next?'

'I thought while they are still at their damned rehearsal we might have a word with Harrison's assistant. Then I suppose we'd better talk to Cross.'

'The black?'

'Don't say things like that,' said Superintendent Nichols.

# CHAPTER X

*Sinfonia Domestica*

Nichols stood in Gaylene's dressing-room with Bob, the assistant stage-door-keeper, soon to be promoted to stage-door-keeper, short, sandy-haired, with an air of being somewhat put-upon, perhaps a consequence of working under Sergeant Harrison. The two men were looking once again at the little device of wires which was obliging so many choral societies in the North and Midlands to begin casting around for a new contralto for their Christmas *Messiah*. Bob shook his head.

'Oh, it was simple enough to *do*,' he said, in answer to a question from Nichols. 'Nothing simpler. Let's see, it was cosy, Wednesday night, wasn't it?' Nichols realized he meant *Così*. 'That means Elizabeth Jenkins would have been here. She'd have been out by eleven or eleven-fifteen, I'd guess—not one to hang about that one. He could have done it then, and hoofed it out the window.'

'Or she,' murmured Nichols.

'Aye, or she,' said Bob. 'Women are up in that sort of thing these days. Come to that, whoever it was could have done it before Harrison locked up for the night, and then just left the theatre in the usual way.'

'True,' said Nichols. 'And I suppose it's just possible that he noticed that someone was much later than usual.'

'Could be,' said Bob, rather dubiously, 'though it's not easy to be that precise about when they're likely to go home. They're theatre people, and I gather that night was a bit special, what with all the cheering and congratulations and so on.'

'Sergeant Harrison wouldn't have gone round checking all the dressing-rooms before he locked the stage-door finally?'

Here Bob frowned. 'I doubt it. He probably wouldn't have checked the principals' dressing-rooms, because he was very particular about noticing them as they went, and saying good-night, so there was no need to see if they were still there. He might have checked some of the others. He might very well have checked up on the principals' dressing-rooms next morning. These rooms are only cleaned once a week—economy like—' here Bob winked—'so he usually made sure things were reasonably ship-shape for whoever was using the room that day, especially if it was one of his favourites.'

'I suppose Miss Ffrench wouldn't have been one of his favourites, though?'

'No, of course she wasn't,' said Bob. 'Can't imagine she was anyone's favourite. Even her mother must have wondered what hit her. Still, she and Sergeant H. jogged along quite nicely, and she never gave him the wrong side of her tongue that I heard. And I *would* have heard, and so would she, I can tell you.'

'He didn't stand any nonsense from the company?'

'Not him. Nor from the audience either, or the fans. He was a real old army man, was Harrison.'

'So in fact there was a very real chance that he would have checked the dressing-rooms yesterday morning before Miss Ffrench or any of the others arrived?'

'Yes—a much better than even chance, I'd say. On the other hand, he got those little bouts of malaria fairly frequently, and he usually felt them coming on in advance. He could have mentioned that to somebody—he did to me, so I knew he might be off yesterday.'

'You didn't hear him mention it to anyone else?'

'No, I didn't. But our times didn't overlap more than a couple of hours on Wednesday, and most of that time I was down in the basement, doing a spot of carpentry—repair work and so on. And Sergeant H. kept to his office—the one you've got now—as he usually did. So he could have told anyone.'

'People dropped by and talked to him, as a rule, did they?'

'Not exactly that, because he wasn't really the chatty type. But they had to go into the office to collect their mail, and any messages. He was very strict about his room: if he wasn't there, it was locked, and they'd have to come back later when he was there. He said that was necessary because of all the lost property there, but to my way of thinking it's just a lot of junk, so if I'm on duty I don't worry all that much. In fact Miss Ffrench had been nosing around there just before her number was called.'

'Yes,' said Nichols, 'she picked up a letter. But normally she wouldn't be able to do that?'

'No, not unless Sergeant H. was off the whole day. As a rule I'd follow his example if I thought he might pop in at any time and catch me out—he could really blow you up if he felt like it. The usual thing was that they'd stop by and ask for post, or Harrison or I would call out to them as they passed that there was something for them. Then we might have a chat, or might not, depending on the person. So he could have told anyone about his malaria on Wednesday, and I wouldn't know about it.'

'Either way,' said Nichols, 'it was a bloody dangerous way of doing somebody in.' The humour of the phrase struck him, and he amended it: 'Slap-happy. Didn't mind if he did someone else in in the course of his nasty little tricks, so long as he eventually got Gaylene Ffrench. For a start, Sergeant Harrison could have seen the doormat outside the dressing-room, smelt a rat, and started investigating.'

'He could,' said Bob. 'There were one or two of those around the theatre—it's a mucky town, Manchester. But that's a pretty funny place to have one. On the other hand it's a nasty dark corridor.'

'Still, a really ruthless sort of mind.'

'That's what gets me,' said Bob. 'Think of there being someone like that around in the company. And it could be any one of about a hundred and fifty. Gives you the shakes.'

'It doesn't make us very happy,' said Superintendent Nichols. 'Right, I think I've got the picture now. But if you think of anything Sergeant Harrison did or said in the last few days that was at all out of the ordinary—come straight to me. And don't on any account say a word to anyone else first.'

'You must think I'm up the ruddy wall,' said Bob. 'I find it difficult enough to pass the time of day with them, in case one of them gets the wrong idea and slits my throat.'

As he went, Superintendent Nichols went back to the little dressing-table. The fingerprint boys had done their work on the room, and on the letter Gaylene had received before her untimely electrification. Now it was lying there. It was from her agent, telling her that the BBC was interested to know if she would be available next year to sing at the last night of the Proms. What play Gaylene would have made with it at the rehearsal, if she had lived to be there! But Nichols felt glad that the few remaining English patriots, who suffered greatly, had been spared the ultimate indignity of a sexy performance of 'Rule, Britannia'.

At home, Simon Mulley's slight theatricality of manner left him almost entirely. Like most singers, he liked to eat well and drink well, but he did it without ostentation or ceremony. When he had joined the company he had rented an ugly little detached house in the suburbs of Manchester, with a tiny porch, little bits of ply-wood timbering, and a weedy garden. He and his wife Margaret had brought up most of their furniture, and they had managed to turn its inconveniences and its absurdities into something oddly pleasant and satisfying. Over dinner on the evening of the first full rehearsal he relaxed, gave a proper degree of attention to his food, and as usual enjoyed talking over with his wife the events of the day.

'It must have been a terribly nervy rehearsal,' Margaret Mulley said, thinking at the same time that Simon was more relaxed than for a long time. 'Everyone looking at everyone else, and wondering which it was. Or wasn't it like that?'

'Well, it was certainly no picnic,' Simon admitted. 'But rehearsals with the Ffrench woman around were pretty jumpy as well. You never knew what vulgar insult she'd be coming out with next. So though Caulfield was still around of course, pretending to direct—and how he does *direct*!' he added, with a wicked little smile at his wife, 'still, in a way we seemed to work *together* better today.'

'That's what you value most, isn't it?'

'Working together, as a company? Yes, that's what this business is all about, for me.'

'What about the new girl?'

'The understudy?' Simon chewed a forkful of food, as if trying to find a way of putting his feelings tactfully. 'It's funny, you know: twenty years ago that girl would have gone to music college, got a few oratorio parts under her belt, pushed the bottom of her voice down to make a good chesty boom, and made a respectable career for herself doing *Elijah* and *Messiah* all over the North. And she'd have been perfectly happy, and probably been a useful teacher to boot. These days nothing contents them but going into opera.

Really, opera is about the only industry that's booming in this country.'

'You should worry about that!' said Margaret Mulley. 'But you think she's not fitted?'

'If she works like a demon,' said Simon, 'she might just pass muster—in certain roles. In others she'll never be anything but an embarrassment—to herself and everyone else.'

'Poor thing. Maddalena's not the easiest of parts if you don't take naturally to the stage.'

'No. Of course it's hellish for her, and almost as bad for Calvin. There's not much any of us can do about it, but naturally Caulfield is going about it entirely in the wrong way.'

'Not shouting at her?'

'Sarcasm, the raised voice just short of the shout, nagging—he's really as pathetic a creature as she is.'

'She probably sees him as an ogre.'

'Probably. He just stopped short of being the complete bully today, but he's bound to get worse.'

'Couldn't you take him aside?'

'I'm the last person who could, after the little set-to we had the other day. In any case, I doubt if anyone would have any effect, except the effect of driving him in the opposite direction. You simply can't *tell* a man as unsure of himself as that. Any suggestion is an affront, something that has to be fought.'

'What a shame—to have the last act mucked up, when the rest is going so well.'

'Musically well, anyway,' said Simon. 'And, when Bridget Lander takes over as Gilda it will go much, much better. When you've got good voices

in the main roles and three or four reasonably intelligent actors, nothing Caulfield can do can bring
the thing down completely. In fact, the reviews
will probably call him a "promising young producer", all the basis of our hard work in resisting
his suggestions.'

'That's the way it goes,' said Margaret Mulley.

'Don't I know it,' said Simon, putting his fork
down and smiling across the table.

Later, over dessert, Margaret Mulley asked her
husband what he would have done about Barbara
Bootle.

'Well, not have given her the part, for a start.
You have to be much more careful about under-
studies than Mike Turner seems to have been in
this case. In fact, the best thing would have been
to send straight to London for a replacement as
soon as Gaylene Ffrench died. Natural Madda-
lenas aren't that rare. Granted that we're landed
with her now, she ought to be rehearsed day and
night, kindly, patiently—in the hope that she will
be able to give *some* kind of performance. And if
we then found that she couldn't, well, then we'd
*have* to get on to the agents and get a last-minute
substitute from London or wherever, however expensive it came. You just can't have the last act
ruined.'

'Couldn't someone coach her in private, without Owen Caulfield knowing?'

'Who though? Calvin would be ideal, but the
lad's newly engaged: one could hardly expect him
to give more than the occasional extra rehearsal
to her. Then there's Ricci—but one would certainly not want to turn any girl over to him.'

'And you?'

Simon looked at his wife, suddenly weary.

'I have my responsibilities,' he said.

There was silence.

'Hadn't you better go up?' said Margaret.

'Yes,' said Simon.

He sat a few minutes longer. Margaret had watched him so often at this time that now she hated to look. His rather distinguished face began almost indefinably to collapse, the firm line of his mouth to droop, the eyes to lose their clear, intelligent focus. Suddenly one seemed to notice his greyness, and to remember that he was no more than forty-five. At that moment Simon Mulley looked like a man with no future, only tormenting memories.

He stood up and left the room, without looking again at Margaret. He took the stairs heavily, one by one, and paused at the turn. Then he went on up to the landing, and opened the door to the smallest bedroom. He thought the woman on the bed gave a tiny smile of recognition as he entered. She was lying curled up on the pillow, sucking her thumb, her legs kicking idly at the bedclothes which had nearly all fallen off. Her body was gross and terrible, and no care in the clothing of her could hide the pity of it. Nothing could hide the vacancy of the expression on her face. Her eyes seemed to see the thumb and the pillow, and no more; no doubt her brain could hold the idea of the thumb and the pillow, and no more. The face had once been beautiful, perhaps, but now it was a blank, and a steady stream of saliva ran down her chin and stained the top of her nightdress. As she sucked she made little grunts and moans of contentment.

Simon Mulley looked at her, and smiled, and then gave a little wave. The creature went on sucking her thumb. Then Simon bent down slowly and kissed her.

Owen Caulfield roamed around the rooms of his little flat, while the gramophone on the sideboard played the Sutherland recording of *Rigoletto*. Now and then he tidied the pens and papers, the sketches and plans on his desk into neat piles, set the little ornaments and mementoes on his tables and mantelpiece into position, or glanced at himself in the mirror. He listened to the music, trying to hear what it should be saying to him. Could it be that other people did in fact hear more than he heard? No—that was just ostentation and pretence. Owen put the thought from him abruptly. He loved opera, had loved it since grammar school days. He heard as much as anybody heard.

Suddenly he thought: I should be relaxing. He sat down in the only good armchair, spread himself out in it, and tried to let the music wash over him. For a few moments it filled every corner of his mind. Then, in one corner of his brain it occurred to him to wonder whether he was lonely. Thirty-seven. Looking older. He nearly got up to look in the mirror again, but remembered he was relaxing. Thirty-seven. Never married. Plenty of odd little affairs, of course, but short. So short. Women took him on, took him *up*, rather, for a short time, and then—lost interest. Went on to others. Dropped him. No—not dropped him. Not dropped him.

And as the idea edged its way forward to the front of his mind, he rejected it. These affairs just fizzled out, that was all. Typical theatrical affairs. He laughed nervously out loud. He wasn't lonely— he was a loner: that was the right way to put it. He held that image of himself up before his eyes, inspected it, tried it on for size. He had tremendous inner resources, he took a woman when he needed one, then got rid of her. He was a frontiersman, a man who was happiest carving out his own path.

He liked that image. It had all the simplicity and directness of a children's Saturday morning cinema film. How he had loved them, on those rare occasions when his father had let him go. The image kept him in his chair for a few minutes more, as Sutherland and Milnes poured out their lungs in the vendetta duet. Then all at once another thought occurred to Owen, and he looked around the room. Was it too tidy? Did it look as if he were obsessive? He went around the room again, ruffling the papers on his desk and displacing the ornaments. It would be ridiculous for people to think he was obsessive. If anyone should come.

James McKaid was phoning his wife in Dungannon. He had enjoyed a long, luxurious bath after the rehearsal, eaten well at the best Italian restaurant in Manchester (where he had waved to Giulia Contini and Signor Pratelli, and been mortified by their all too evident uncertainty as to who he was), and had come straight back to his flat which was conveniently close. Now he was sitting in the easiest of easy chairs, with the receiver crooked between his shoulder and his ear, and a stiff glass of whisky convenient to his right hand.

'It went as well as you could expect,' he was saying. 'Jumpy? Yes, of course everyone's jumpy. You couldn't expect anything else, could you? And the Superintendent interviewing people when they were off-stage didn't help . . . Ricci . . . Yes, I shouldn't be surprised . . . He didn't say much when he came out . . . But the rehearsal didn't go too badly, all things considered, and when you remember the limitations of that bunch. The Contini is a great farce of course.' He opened his lungs and sang into the receiver: 'Oh-ee-ah-oo-ai . . . No, nothing but, the whole time! I didn't hear a single consonant. And it's not even much of a voice. So much for engaging a singer on the basis of a few good reviews in *Opera*. Mike Turner should have learnt a thing or two from this little fiasco, anyway . . . Simon? Oh, being the great artist, as usual. I never did think method acting went too well in opera, but grant the approach, grant the approach, it's a perfectly respectable performance.' He took a good gulp of whisky, and closed his eyes. 'Ah yes, our resident black, the living proof of our tolerance and intellectual maturity? A very nice little performance. Very nice. They'll cheer him to the echo, of course. All those long-haired scruffs in the gallery who've been howling at his Rodolfo. They'd cheer Cassius Clay as Tristan, they would: put something in front of them that they think is a challenge to their radical

consciences, and they're off after it like a pack of
demented beagles, however ludicrous it may be.
Still, all in all, Calvin doesn't disgrace the company, though some people might think that faint
praise . . . Will you be coming Thursday? . . . Yes,
I'll meet you if I can . . . Anyway, I'll try and
phone you Sunday—there's no rehearsal then, unless they try and dig a performance out of the
Bootle girl . . . I shan't be involved, anyway . . .
I'll meet you in the car if I can, if not go to Plimsoll Street . . . Right . . . Love you.' And he made
kissing noises into the receiver, and put it back on
its rest.

He took another good mouthful of whisky, then
rummaged in the pocket of the silk dressing-gown
which he had put on when he had got back from
the restaurant. He believed in being comfortable.
He scribbled for some time on the back of an en-
velope, and then looked at the result with satisfaction. Then he took up the phone again, and
dialled. This time he held the receiver to his ear
carefully, and spoke softly into the mouthpiece.

Mike Turner was also relaxing in his enormous
Victorian apartment near the centre of Manchester, and he was relaxing impeccably. He had
showered, and donned cream slacks and a choco-
late-coloured silk shirt. Then he had eaten the
lobster mayonnaise left out for him by his house-
keeper-cook, whom he rarely saw, but who wor-
shipped his smooth good looks in the various
photos of him around the apartment, and who
worried whether he was getting enough to eat.
Then he made himself thick black coffee, lit a

Piccadilly, and walked around the wonderfully spacious expanses of his sitting-room. He looked as if he were advertising the sort of car that everyone foolish envies, and no one sensible can afford.

He walked very elegantly, for smoothness is not something that should be lightly laid aside in private. At times it almost seemed as if he floated. His hands were the liveliest thing about him, for they were conducting, as they had been all afternoon—conducting *Rigoletto*. Parts of the score that particularly pleased him had him singing and conducting with a smile of contentment on his face. Parts that had not gone well that afternoon had him frowning, and trying them over various ways, always humming or growling in imitation of the orchestra. Sometimes he used his cigarette as a baton, and sometimes, especially in a tender passage, he looked at himself in the enormous mirror over the marble mantelpiece.

He had been conducting *Rigoletto* to himself for nearly an hour when another thought struck him, and he took a sheet of paper from the drawer of the desk, seated himself decoratively on a corner, and did various calculations that seemed to mean something to him, to judge by the quizzical raising of the eyebrows, the comically-exaggerated perplexity of his manner.

His smoothness was hardly disturbed by the infinitesimal sound of the opening of the main door of the flat, unexpected though it seemed to be. By the time the door to the sitting-room was opened he was half way across the room.

'Darling,' he said. '*Darling.*'

The flat suddenly seemed filled with spring

flowers, with strawberries and champagne, with the rustle of expensive materials and the taste of exotic meals.

'This is a lovely surprise,' said Mike, to the bringer of all these good things. 'Why on earth didn't you tell me you were coming?'

'To catch you out, of course,' said the splendid creature. 'What sort of wife doesn't *itch* to catch her husband out? It covers a multitude of her own sins.'

'Well, this time,' said Mike, 'you are going to suffer a deep disappointment, I'm afraid, darling.'

And he kissed her again. In the waste-paper basket by the desk lay a crumpled sheet of paper, with a series of calculations in pencil.

# CHAPTER XI

*Black Notes and White Notes*

'Hate her?' said Calvin Cross, spreading out his hands ingenuously and looking at Superintendent Nichols. 'I don't know—one doesn't really think in those terms. But certainly I thought her one of the most ghastly women I've ever met.'

'You quarrelled, I gather,' said Nichols.

Calvin frowned briefly. 'Ah—someone's been talking. Who, I wonder? Well, again, quarrelled isn't quite the word for it, because we didn't have stand-up slanging-matches of the sort some members of the company go in for. It was more a matter of guerrilla warfare—of her lobbing neat little bombs in my direction, and me fielding them and lobbing them back. The fact is that we were sniping at each other, or niggling each other in some way, pretty much the whole time.'

Calvin's pleasant, boyish face was open and transparent, his smile ready, his look steady. He seemed the frankest of frank witnesses, and Nichols found himself wondering what lay behind it, wondering if anything was being covered up, if another self lurked behind the white teeth and engaging smile. Because no one grew up black in

Britain without bruises, little emotional wounds that could be cherished and nourished, and picked at until they became gaping holes. No black could be quite as *genuine* with a policeman as Calvin Cross was trying to be—it would go against his whole experience as an immigrant.

'Was it just a matter of colour, this bad feeling between the two of you?' Nichols asked.

'Colour?' said Calvin. 'Oh, someone's told you about *that* little incident, have they? Owen, I suppose. No, no—that didn't come till we were well-entrenched enemies. I suppose you could say that our differences were mainly artistic.

'You mean you had different approaches to the opera?' asked Nichols.

'That's one way of putting it,' said Calvin, his face becoming suddenly serious. 'You see, we've got Simon Mulley as Rigoletto. I don't know if you've heard of him, but the only thing to be said, really, is that he's a great artist. Bridget and I are watching him every minute of rehearsals, every gesture he makes, just learning from him the whole time—quite apart from the singing, and what he can do with a simple phrase—it's just unbelievable.'

Calvin pulled himself up.

'Sorry—you won't want me getting all enthusiastic. But the fact is, working with him is a great experience for young singers like us. He's marvellous to us: we all three talk over the opera a lot— our parts, the movements, and so on. Most of the time we have to fight Owen Caulfield to get to do what we want, but that's by the way. The point is that the three of us—and Ricci, too—are really trying to do justice to the piece, if that doesn't sound too pompous.'

'Not at all,' said Nichols. 'I get your point. And I suppose Miss Ffrench wasn't interested in this sort of approach.'

'Miss Ffrench was only interested in waggling her tits in the audience's face. She was interested in sex and herself, and that was absolutely all. Other considerations simply didn't get through to her. Bellow out the music in any old style at all, and throw your body around so that everyone spends their time mentally undressing you and ignoring anything else that might be happening on stage—that was the sum total of her ideas on how to present opera.'

'So you felt she didn't fit in to the production as it was developing?' asked Nichols.

'That's putting it mildly. But she was sleeping with Owen, or had been. And he wanted her back. So he more or less went along with anything she did—he wasn't managing to get much style into the production anyway, so you couldn't say she went against any of his notions.'

'You say he wanted her back?'

Calvin's face said: 'Sorry I said that. Ignore it.'

'Well, that's what we thought,' he said. 'We might have been wrong.'

'Were you and Miss Ffrench completely hostile from the beginning,' asked Nichols, 'or did she display some . . . interest early on?'

'Well, I'd say she cast the appraising eye over me,' said Calvin ruefully. 'But there's hardly a man in the company she didn't do that to, except perhaps Mr. Pettifer. She made the odd tentative advance in my direction—no, not tentative: blatant. But in fact we didn't hit it off right from the beginning, so there was nothing doing.'

'Considerations like that don't seem to have inhibited some of the others,' murmured Nichols.

'Well, no. But we passed from distant politeness to sniping in a matter of twenty-four hours. And Bridget had just arrived too, and she and I were already getting interested in each other, even then. So I escaped her much-patronized bed.'

'You don't think your . . . colour would have prevented it, if you'd been inclined?'

'If I'd been bright purple and a hunch-back cripple I'd have made it. There were rights of unlimited access there.'

'But what about Miss Ffrench's reaction when you got engaged?' asked Nichols. 'I understand that this was based on the fact that Miss Lander was white and you were black.'

Calvin paused before answering, looking at his hands. 'I think I understand that better now,' he said finally. 'I don't honestly think that had much to do with—with colour prejudice or whatever you like to call it. Frankly, as I suppose you realize, she had just the nastiest goddam mind of anyone I've ever known. She just loved being unpleasant, and she'd grab any weapon to hand. I mean, if I *had* been a cripple, she'd have called me that. If I'd had a squint, she'd have called me "cross-eyes". It was just a case of the nearest and bluntest instrument.'

'But you didn't think along these lines at the time, sir?'

Calvin, caught up short, gave his engaging grin. 'Well, no, I didn't. I was pretty mad. As I expect you've heard. But you know you can't stay like that for very long. If you let that sort of feeling get a hold of you, you start going in for Black Muslimism, Afro hair-cuts and natty robes. And I can do without cold legs. I wouldn't want to stop being a human being and start up as a professional Black. I'll save that till I lose my voice and need to pick up a bit of money giving television interviews.'

Nichols looked at this rather sophisticated young man, and wondered if his blackness hadn't left a larger residue of resentment and hurt pride than he pretended.

'And there's another thing,' said Calvin.

'Yes?'

'Well, she just loved publicity. Of course we all do, anyone on stage, and don't believe anyone who tells you different. But to her it was a drug, an absolute mania. It gets some people that way: they think it can do all sorts of things for you, a sort of wonder drug that changes you from the second to the first-rate. Gaylene not only wanted as much as she could get herself, but she hated other people getting it. I think part of her reaction to Bridget and me getting engaged was just that: she didn't want us getting our picture in the papers.'

'Could she have known you would?' asked Nichols sceptically.

'Oh yes. She knew the reporters would go liberal soft-centred over us—she knew all the ins and outs of the publicity game. I expect she was planning to make a big splash when Hurtle pitched up, and then we scooped the pool in advance—trumped her ace, so to speak.'

'And I suppose when the attempts on her life began—'

'Yes—I assumed she'd overtrumped our trump. But of course one always had to take into account the possibility of the attacks being genuine. As I said to Bridget: this is one murder one doesn't have to look for a motive for, Gaylene being what she was.'

It was a potentially damaging admission, given out with the utmost frankness. Nichols wondered whether anyone so sophisticated could be quite so ingenuous and open as Calvin was trying to seem. His experience told him not.

'I'm not at all sure about it being unnecessary to look for a motive,' said Nichols, 'though I take your point about how generally unpleasant she made herself. But, you know, people who murder other people don't do it for *dislike*, not if they're sane. There are plenty of pretty repellent people walking the streets, whom lots of people would enjoy sticking the bread-knife in to. But they don't do it. Either we've got a madman on our hands— and so far it doesn't look that way to me—or we need something in the way of motive much stronger than I've heard of so far.'

'I'm sure you're right as a general rule, Superintendent,' said Calvin. 'But of course you never met Gaylene.'

'Were you performing on the night before Miss Ffrench died?' asked Nichols, with one of the abrupt changes of subject he enjoyed springing on people.

'No—but I was in the theatre.'

'Oh?'

'Bridget was having her big triumph in *Così*. That's *Così Fan Tutte*—Mozart, you know. I watched her from the gallery, then I went backstage afterwards.'

'And after that?' asked Nichols. 'Did you stay with Miss Lander for some time?'

'About half an hour or so. She had to go off for drinks with Mike Turner and a local money-bags. I went on to her flat and waited for her.'

'About what time would that mean you left the theatre?'

'About eleven-twenty or eleven-thirty I imagine. You could check with Serg—oh no. Christ, that was nasty. That really made me sick.'

'It's the murder of Harrison,' said Nichols, 'that makes us think this isn't just a matter of theatrical rivalries and jealousies. Where were you last night?'

'Last night? I did a bit of work on *Rigoletto* with Bridget and Giulia Contini. Helping her to get her words, trying to get her to do a bit of acting— though frankly that's beyond me, and everyone else. I went back to my flat about nine or so.'

'I see,' said Nichols. 'When you left the theatre on Wednesday night, did you talk to Harrison about the *Così* performance?'

'Nothing much. Just "wasn't it great?" or something like that.'

'But you did talk to him.'

'Yes, but only the odd word,' said Calvin. 'I always rather thought wogs were there to be ruled with rod and gun in Sergeant Harrison's opinion. But he was a nice chap. And he didn't do much more than pass the time of day with most of the other members of the company.'

'So I gathered,' said Nichols. 'You think if he'd seen something on Wednesday night, he would have kept quiet about it.'

'I'm sure he would. If he noticed anything at all, he'd either have chewed it over to himself, which is most likely, because he was a slow sort of chap, and then had it out with whoever it was. Or else he would have gone to his commanding officer.'

'Meaning?'

'Mike Turner.'

'I did ask him after Harrison's murder, but he says not. It would more or less have to have been by phone, because Harrison didn't come in on Thursday.'

'True,' said Calvin. 'Well, I'd have thought that unless it was the sort of thing he felt he ought to go to the police with, the only other person he'd talk it over with would be Mike. He believed in a chain of command—a real old Kipling character was Harrison.'

'That was my impression over the phone,' said Nichols. 'Well, I don't think I need keep you any longer, sir. I presume you'll be around if you're wanted?'

'There's only about a week to first night,' said Calvin. 'You bet I'll be around.'

He got up from his chair, gave one of his engaging grins, and left the stage-door office.

'Nice enough lad,' said Sergeant Chappell.

'Very nice,' said Nichols. 'Rather a contrast to Mr. Caulfield, I thought.'

'But he was acting,' said Sergeant Chappell.

'Oh yes,' said Nichols. 'He was acting.'

Outside in the corridor Calvin, having shut the door behind him, leaned for a moment his forehead against the doorpost. He felt exhausted. Completely done in. It's all that acting, he said to himself. I'm tired to death of acting.

The weekend was spent in routine of the most soul-destroying kind, of checking and counter-checking, interviewing and phoning, most of it in connection with the alibi cards handed in by every member of the company. Nichols also managed to pay a visit to the tall, dignified Victorian house which had housed Gaylene during her brief career in Manchester.

While Nichols and a couple of constables examined the contents of Gaylene's flat—the massive array of lotions, creams, moisturizers, powders, mascaras and scents, the wardrobe of scanty clothes for a hefty body, the dog-eared women's magazines of the kind which assumes its readers to have neither mind nor taste—Sergeant Chappell was talking to the couple who lived downstairs. Their views, he thought, would have the advantage of being uncoloured by professional jealousy. Be that as it may, they found it something of a struggle to dredge up a single good word to say for her.

'Of course, we wouldn't want to speak ill of the dead,' said Mrs Hogben, itching to and intending to, 'and she may have been a very good-natured girl at heart for all we know, but, you see, Bert and I aren't used to that sort of thing, are we Bert? And it gives the house a bad name. It's not as though she was discreet about it.'

'Discreet?' put in Bert. 'She wouldn't know the meaning of the word.'

'She broadcast it from the housetops, if you get my meaning,' said Mrs Hogben.

'Men?' suggested Sergeant Chappell.

'Well, it certainly wasn't hamsters,' said Bert Hogben.

'A whole string of them, one after another,' said Mrs Hogben. 'You hardly ever saw the same face twice in a row. And the noise they made about it! D'you know, I don't think I've once heard her go up those stairs with a chap but she's bellowed something down to him, so everyone in the house could hear. But it wasn't so much the noise, it was the sort of things she shouted . . . !'

'Crude?'

'I wouldn't sully the air by repeating them. Well, once I couldn't stand it any more, and I went out to the landing and I said: "Miss Ffrench," I said (and where she got that second little f except out of thin air I'd like to know), "Miss Ffrench," I said, "we're not used to that sort of language in this house," I said.'

'What did she say?' asked Sergeant Chappell.

'Well, she just looked at me like I'd just crawled out of the woodwork and you know I really don't think she knew what I was talking about. Anyway, she just turned and went up the stairs, and bellowed "some silly old git" to the chap that was with her. I complained to the landlord, naturally, but you just can't get rid of people these days, not even these squatters, can you? so I might as well have spared my breath.'

'And the noises from upstairs,' put in Bert. 'Well —you've heard about those dirty tape-recordings they sell, haven't you? Well, we could have made a few down here in this flat—made a packet we could've. Made your hair curl sometimes, and I was in the Navy.'

'What about the night she fell downstairs?' asked Sergeant Chappell. 'Did you hear that?'

'Well, of course we more or less picked her up,' said Mrs Hogben. 'We heard this terrible bumping, and we came out, and she was lying on the floor over there, bellowing and shouting and creating blue murder. But she wasn't much hurt, and frankly we didn't set too much store by it, not when we'd talked it over.'

'Why not?'

'Well,' said Mrs Hogben, lowering her voice as if about to reveal something yet more scandalous than hitherto. 'She smelt, if you catch my meaning. She'd been *drinking* in her room. Then she tried to come down the stairs in the dark (which she *needn't* have done, because she could have left her door open, then come and switched on the landing light down here)—anyway, as I was saying, she tripped up and went bottom over head, so to speak. We felt sure that's what must have happened. It wasn't till after she . . . passed away that we went up and found the drawing pins on the fifth step down.'

They all looked up to where the police themselves had earlier noted the tell-tale pins, one of them with a little bit of knotted thread still attached.

'But there had been another attempt before—and in this house, hadn't there?' asked Sergeant Chappell.

'So we *read*,' said Mrs Hogben.

'It's just her word, isn't it?' said Bert.

'You don't think anybody could have come into the house in the night and turned the gas on?'

'I don't know about that,' said Mrs Hogben. 'Where there's locks there's ways of opening locks. All I say is, when people drink like that, secret-like, in their own homes, they do funny things. I mean, it's not like a drink in a pub, is it?—though personally I'm temperance, always have been—but when you take it in your own home, a girl of that age, and drinking whisky . . .'

The sentence was left hanging in the musty air of the dim landing, but Mrs Hogben's expression of pinched disapproval seemed to say that all was up with a girl who could do that.

'Well,' said Chappell, 'you could be right. But it's a long staircase for someone to arrange to fall down.'

They all looked up the dark Victorian expanse of stairs—narrow, steep, ill-lit, the last long trek of the nineteenth-century housemaid after a fifteen-hour day.

'Maybe,' said Mrs Hogben defiantly. 'But *she* only had a few bruises, as far as we could see.'

'I'm sorry,' said Chappell, 'but we've got to take it more seriously than that—seeing the jokester finally got her.'

' 'Ere,' said Bert Hogben, his shaggy grey moustache bobbing with detective zeal, 'how's this for an idea? She sets this 'ere booby trap for someone else, then gets caught in it herself!'

Sergeant Chappell explained how unlikely it was that Gaylene, having electrified the doorknob, would have put her own hand within a hundred yards of it before she was quite sure the connection had been broken.

'Pity,' said Mrs Hogben, shaking her head, 'because it would have been so neat, and she did have it coming to her. And whoever did it, I'd hate to see him actually suffer for it.'

It seemed to Sergeant Chappell that no murderer had enjoyed such universal public sympathy since the gentlemen who robbed the Russian Imperial family of the counsels of Gregory Rasputin.

# CHAPTER XII

## *Tutti*

Giulia Contini had accepted her present engagement to improve her English. As she talked to Nichols at the back of the stalls, with the menacing, ambiguous opening chords of *Rigoletto* swelling around them, it didn't seem to Nichols that she could have done so. On the other hand, it was clear that she had had to revise her opinions of the English.

'Is said ze English is cold,' she said, smiling genially and waving her hands, 'is correct, polite, all ziss ting. But I never see so emotion! Shoutings, rowings—and now ziss! Murder—two murder! Real nasty murderings!'

Signor Pratelli, who was sitting beside her watching over her like a child prodigy's mother, interposed with a florid sentence in which Nichols could detect the words '*assassino*' and '*uccide*' and a great many implied exclamation marks.

'Quite,' he said.

'Zey say we 'Talians are emotion pipple,' said Giulia seriously. 'But we 'ave our bit crying, bit shouting, bit loving—then pouf! all gone! But 'ere is not like. 'Ere nobody forget, nobody kiss and good friend again. They goes on and on wid dair nasty tempers, and spiteness and quarrellings. Is not nice.'

'You felt the atmosphere, did you, even before Miss Ffrench died?' asked Nichols.

'Si, si, was *evidente*,' said Giulia. 'I not complaining. Is nice pipple here too. Bridget and Calvin and lots more, is very nice to me, helps me, jolly kind. But that Guylene—she sets them all—what you say?—topsy turvey, wrong side up, she makes them not nice, she makes nasty atmosphere all round 'er, like a bad smell'

She wrinkled her nose expressively. Signor Pratelli, to justify his manager's fees, put in a few words—'*squaldrina*', '*abandonata*' and '*stupida*'—which convinced Nichols he was talking about Gaylene.

'*Si, si, capito*,' said Nichols, in some embarrassment. This feeble gesture released a flood of Italian emotion, which seemed to spring from a feeling that this murder was bad for his protégée's career, and perhaps that association with murderers and criminals of that sort was something perilous for her soul.

'*Basta!*' said Giulia contemptuously. But it was not.

Nichols let his attention wander towards the stage, where the curtain had risen to display an economical but handsome ducal court. Calvin and Bridget were playing out their brief scene together: the court band was playing in the background, and Calvin was establishing his character as the noble seducer by laying siege to the Countess Ceprano: 'You leave us? How cruel . . .' His tones were honeyed and passionate, sometimes sinking to a near-whisper, and Bridget's replies were reluctant and full of wistful regret. A sexual tension filled the theatre, and the courtiers around them on the stage, led by Jim McKaid as Marullo, looked on with ironic admiration. In McKaid's case this seemed to embrace a barely concealed sneer.

'*Basta!*' said Giulia Contini again to Signor Pratelli who was still in full flood.

'*Si, si, carina,*' he said placatingly.

Simon Mulley was now coming to the centre of the stage to bait the Countess's husband, but Nichols tore his attention regretfully from the stage.

'You didn't quarrel with Miss Ffrench yourself, did you?' he said to Giulia.

'I not quarrel with nobodys,' said Giulia. 'I come, I play few performances, I go—is nothing to me. I ignore. She try to make friends, but I ignore. Was vulgar, *brutta, stupida.*' She curled her mouth round the words, and her face, heavy with stage make-up, seemed to crease up with exaggerated disgust. 'Is others I was sorry for. To work with 'er, weeks and months. *Impossibile!*'

'You were coming among these people for the first time,' said Nichols. 'Would you say that relationships were so bad that you could understand Miss Ffrench being murdered?'

Giulia thought for a bit, then turned to Signor Pratelli and launched into a long conversation in which Nichols distinguished the words '*brutto affaro*', '*infame*' and '*atroce*' and had twice to protect himself from flailing hands. Finally Giulia Contini turned back to him.

'No,' she said.

Nichols waited for her to go on, but she didn't.

'Why do you say no?' he finally asked.

'Because ordinary pipples, they doesn't murders,' she said. 'Is needing more—what you say?—motives. If I murders everybodies I dislikes in opera companies—*Dio mio!*' She grinned ecstatically, but when Signor Pratelli interjected what seemed to be a caution, she turned on him with a look which suggested that his name would probably be included on her list of victims.

'*Tacete!*' she hissed.

It seemed as well to let them go. The scene had changed, the Duke's palace had vanished into the flies, and they were now outside Rigoletto's house. Soon Giulia would be wanted as Gilda, and Nichols gestured her towards the stage. Signor Pratelli trotted in her wake, for all the world as if he was intending to play her confidante. On stage Raymond Ricci was offering his service as hired assassin to Simon Mulley as Rigoletto. His oily, insinuating deportment was as cleverly repulsive as ever, and his saturnine appearance as menacing. At the crucial moment in the scene when the offer is made he began fingering the edge of his short sword, as an earnest of his abilities with the knife. Was it Nichols's imagination, or did he detect in Raymond Ricci's acting at this point a certain hesitancy? A certain embarrassment? And could it possibly be the result of a certain memory?

'Mr Ritchie?' said Raymond Ricci's landlady, on her doorstep in her hair-curlers, her eyes glazed with housework, and looking the dead spit of the unfortunate Florrie Capp. 'Yes, that's right, he was away on Wednesday night. Got an engagement somewhere abroad. I remember because I'd done him some spaghetti, him being Italian, and I'd just put on the potatoes to go with it when 'is brother came in and told me—they're both with me, you know, but the other doesn't eat, like, does for himself, more independent. So he'd already gone off, by plane to wherever it was, one of these places, you know, and so it was a bit wasted, like.'

PC Lyme, one of several policemen footslogging around Manchester on the impossible task of checking up alibis, nodded his pleasant middle-aged head and asked: 'Is Ricci a good type of lodger?'

"Ee, they're nice as pie, both of 'em. No trouble at all. Course they're close. To each other, like. They're Italians, really, aren't they? And they are that way—clannish, you know. I like to see it myself. It's not like my kids: my Syd won't speak to my Daphne, they're at sixes and sevens every time they come round, mind you, I blame Syd's wife . . .'

'So you've no complaints?' put in PC Lyme quickly.

'Bless you, no. I mean, if there's a woman now and then it's only human nature, and rather that than something else, and we're not in the nineteeth century, are we? Let 'em have a bit of fun, I say, because it's no fun being married, not in my experience. I'm all for theatre people myself. They bring a bit of life into the house, don't they?'

Or a bit of death, thought PC Lyme.

\* \* \*

Jim McKaid perched on the back of the stalls seat, his feet on the row in front. He didn't look casual, but casualness was obviously his aim. Before long he would be called to kidnap Gilda from her father's house, but now the voices of Simon Mulley and Giulia Contini were flooding through the theatre, contrasting oddly in their fullness with the pinched, cynical, bored-tolerant expression on the face of McKaid.

'Of course I realize that being in bed with Gaylene at the time of the gas-attack is hardly what you'd call an alibi,' he said, twisting his mouth into a man-to-man smile at Nichols. 'Still, I assure you the experience was so nasty—the *gassing*, I mean, of course—nasty *and* bad for the voice, that when I *do* decide to kill somebody in that way I'll make sure I don't stay around.'

Nichols made the instant appraisal of McKaid that almost everyone made—that there was something about him he didn't like. He tried to keep the thing as businesslike as possible.

'It's perhaps as good an alibi as any in some ways,' he said. 'What about for the night before she died . . . I see from your card that you were on stage here.'

'That's right. Alfonso in *Così*. Mozart, you know. Lovely little piece. Alfonso is the best part in the whole opera, really, though the lovers get all the fireworks. I'm rather surprised Mr Turner entrusts me with it.' Again the lopsided smile.

'And after the performance?'

'Had a drink to toast Bridget. Because really she is a *very* promising little singer. Then I went home. Alone. And to bed, alone. Sorry—I'm alibi-less.'

'Did you say good night to Sergeant Harrison on the way out?'

'If he was at the stage-door I probably did. Not the kind of thing one would remember, is it? Especially after a glass or two.'

'Going back to the previous attempt—the gas: what exactly happened? You woke up, I suppose, and the room was full of gas?'

'That's right. I started coughing and spluttering, woke, realized something was wrong, and rolled over towards Gaylene. We both staggered up and threw the windows open.'

'Would you have said you woke in the nick of time?'

'Wouldn't know. It's not the sort of thing one acquires experience of, being gassed. But it's an old house, draughty, so I'd guess it would take a fair while. I suspect it was done in the early morning and that it would have taken another hour or so before we handed in our cards. Probably more with Gaylene—she had a marvellous pair of lungs. Or would that make it quicker?'

'At any rate, you were both all right after a bit?'

'A bit groggy, but not too bad. She was spared to raise merry hell for a few days more, and I was spared to adorn the vital and distinguished role of Marullo, whom everyone forgets as soon as the curtain falls. To which part I must return.'

And as he leapt over the seat and strolled towards the stage, as Giulia Contini, alone on the stage and making one of the little gestures with the left hand which were her tribute to dramatic art, was emitting the tentative shakes that passed for the trills that should adorn the aria 'Caro nome'.

Even as McKaid walked, he seemed to carry his grudge crouching like a malignant monkey on one shoulder.

PC Lyme had watched Hurtle alternately jogging and sprinting around the seemingly infinite length of the running track where he was training, and finally come not to rest, but to a settled position a hundred or so yards away, where he first ran energetically up and down on the spot, then with sweeping, swooping movements like a hulking bird threw his right hand over his head and brought it down to touch his left toe, and then did the same for his left hand and right toe. As PC Lyme approached him he seemed oblivious of his presence, and commenced a series of motions apparently designed to break his back, motions which made it very difficult for PC Lyme to decide whether to approach him from behind or in front, and suggested to him that only by his doing a handstand could they manage to talk with both their heads up the same way.

'Mr Marwick?' he said finally, as Hurtle's face appeared between his legs and seemed to register Lyme's blue serge legs.

'Call me Hurtle,' said Hurtle, in what seemed a Pavlovian response. Then he stretched up to the heavens and began twisting around the upper-half of his trunk in a bewildering snake-like way, making any attempt to meet him face to face out of the question.

'I have a message from Superintendent Nichols,' shouted Lyme.

'Chappie I sent the times and dates to,' said

Hurtle, not seeming at all winded, but putting one hand on a hip and lurching to the right to touch the ground from the side. 'Hope it was all OK. 'Fraid there wasn't anything much they could check on. We don't get about much when we're in training.' He swooped once more down towards his toes, which were taking a terrible punishment. ''Course, when the tour's over, it'll be different.' He grinned briefly in passing into PC Lyme's face. 'London'll never be the same again, that's for sure!'

Giving up the useless task of trying to address him head on, PC Lyme shouted in his most stentorian policeman's voice: 'Nichols would like to see you. Tonight.'

'Can't be done,' said Hurtle, taking to running on the spot again. 'Got a game—kick-off at seven-thirty?'

'Could you make half past five? At the theatre?' shouted Lyme, resisting the temptation to jog in unison.

'Do me level,' said Hurtle. 'Want to do all I can to help. 'Course, you see his point of view—chappie who did it. But still, she was a Coona girl. No Pom's going to do in a Coona girl and get away with it, not if I can help it!'

And he took off at an unmatchable speed around the track, shouting over his shoulder: 'Tell Nichols she'll be right. Five-thirty on the dot.'

The dress rehearsal was nearing its end. Nichols, who had kept half an eye on it throughout his questioning, was now riveted by the interplay of personalities, on stage and off. Owen, until now, had tried to interrupt the action as little as possible, generally confining himself to pep-talks after each scene, thus acknowledging that at least parts of the action had passed out of his control. Nichols was fascinated to hear the tone of the pep-talk—bluff, jocular, friendly, chiding, but with an undertone of sarcasm, bullying, contempt—so that suddenly one saw under the thick protective shell of the producer in full command the traces of some strange emotional wound whose cause and nature one could only guess at.

Now the last act was beginning, and Owen announced in advance that he might have to interrupt more in the course of the act, since Barbara Bootle 'might have some difficulties fitting herself in to the new production'. It might have been tactfully meant. One never knew with Owen how far he was conscious of the undertones in what he said, how far he could anticipate the sort of reactions his words would arouse. But certainly they had the effect of making Barbara more nervous still, and she stood in the wings a ridiculous spectacle—a heavy, substantial girl in a blue funk.

After the stifled opening exchanges of Rigoletto, and Gilda, Calvin produced a 'La donna è mobile' of supreme elegance and wicked charm. It did not lighten the heart of Barbara, for this was her moment. She walked on to the stage and over it as if she were going before a firing squad, with an unconvinced show of defiance. She was attempting to swing her hips, as she had been told to do many times, but the motion resembled more a convulsive jerk. It was only when she opened her mouth that one had the idea that there might be anything in her at all to counterbalance the hideous embarrassment of her stage presence. Shut your eyes, Nichols thought to himself, and this girl might really be something. Even then, though, the impression was mixed: for a couple of phrases the voice would ring out rich, clear and characterful; then it would seem as if she had drawn a heavy velvet curtain over it and it would lose all its immediacy—no doubt it was the vocal equivalent of the heavy velvet curtain she heartily desired could separate the audience from her acting performance.

Calvin did his best: when he clasped her hand passionately he put his body between her and a good three-quarters of the auditorium, though he hoped that on the first night she would not allow the remaining quarter to see the very obvious expression of gratitude on her face. As the seduction advanced towards the moment where the great quartet begins he, by arrangement, managed to push her further down on to the rough inn bench, so that the audience could see little more of her than her legs giving kicks of mock protest. It was odd how unconvincing Barbara could make even a kick. When they got to the quartet Owen stopped them.

'Very nice, Calvin, very nice,' he said, with that geniality that froze gratitude. 'Now, Barbara, your problem is the beginning isn't it?—getting on to the stage. We all realize your problem, all of us here, because the first time is never easy. You've got to learn to let your body *go*, not to . . . well, never mind. I want you to do it from the beginning again, and I want you to relax your whole body in the wings, completely relax, then walk over naturally—naturally, forget the seductive walk for the mo-

ment—then stand by the table with your hand on
your hip. You can do a three-quarters turn away
from the audience if it makes you feel any easier.
Then Calvin can get you down on the bench as
before. OK, Barbara?'

Barbara nodded miserably. Everyone went back
to first positions, and Mike began the scene again.
It had been perfectly sensible advice as far as it
went, but the patience was exaggerated, and as
Barbara stood in the wings she remembered only
that 'well, never mind', and she mulled over to herself the variety of wounding phrases it could have
been designed to hide. She was a Lancashire girl,
and she hated sarcasm, as she hated condescension,
and she stiffened with resentment. When her moment came she marched purposefully forward,
which at any rate came nearer to a natural walk
than her whore's wiggle, took up her station by the
table, and put her hand stiffly but firmly on her hip.
At that moment Owen's high, irritated voice rose
over the scurrying strings:

'Seductively, for God's sake. Do it seductively.
You look like an arthritic charwoman.'

The orchestra continued, Calvin continued, but
there was a blank in the mezzo line. Gradually all
the music faded away, and a large, rich Lancashire
voice was heard:

'What did you say?'

'I said do it seductively,' said Owen, his own
voice rising and containing notes of the now fa-
miliar tantrums.

'After that. What did you say after that?'

'I said you looked like an arthritic charwoman,'

said Owen, his anger totally getting the better of his caution.

Barbara Bootle blushed a violent red, and turned on him.

'That was *bloody* rude. You'll take that back. I know I'm no good, and I'd rather die than do this part, but you make me twice as bad because you're such a bully and make me feel such a worm, and I'm not putting up with any more of your sneers, or any of your snide insinuations—nor any of your condescension for that matter.'

Barbara was transformed. For the moment everyone in the theatre forgot the lumpy, self-conscious body and noted only the glint in the eye and the set of the shoulders. It was the voice of indedependent Lancashire they had been hearing, the sort of voice whose dogged unreason echoed through Trade Union Congresses and caused little quakes of panic in the hearts of Ministry of Labour conciliators. But it was clear that Owen was not bent on conciliation.

'Who the hell do you think you're talking to?' he shouted, his voice beginning to bray, as it always did when he felt himself challenged. 'And who the hell do you think you are? I'm running this rehearsal and it's my job to get some sort of performance out of you.' He paused, and then suddenly seemed to throw his whole body at her, as if totally possessed by his own rage. 'AND I MEAN TO GET IT IF I HAVE TO KNOCK IT IN TO YOU.' His face was red, his eyes protruding, his hands gesticulating jerkily. Barbara's courage seemed to be failing her a little, though it had by no means deserted her.

'You won't get any kind of performance out of me by behaving like a pig,' she said stoutly.

'A pig!' bellowed Owen. 'What the hell kind of language is that? I'm the producer of this damned opera, and I've had nothing but opposition and arguments the whole time—all through rehearsals— not an ounce of cooperation or willingness, and now you come along, you *bloody* little incompetent, and you turn in the sort of performance that would make a village concert-party cringe to look at you, and then you have the hide to turn around on me and . . .'

'Pig—*si!*' said a voice suddenly from the back of the stage. *'Gran' bestia! Fascist! Piccolo Mussolini! E brrrrutto! No mi piace qui! E finito per me!'*

Mike Turner, from his podium, looked aghast at the plump little form of Giulia Contini, which had come to the front of the stage hands on hips, shoulders heaving, looking for all the world like a Neapolitan housewife whose butcher has sold her horse-meat for beef. Giulia was livid with a quite disinterested rage, a primitive sort of female chivalry. It was clear that her last words were a threat of departure. Mike saw himself losing the star of his show, and all the money already paid to her. Mike, for all his smoothness, was very good in an emergency. He turned to Owen.

'You're fired,' he said. 'As of now.'

Owen, who had been frozen into an apoplectic posture by the interruption, suddenly crumpled down into his seat, his head forward on the back of the row in front, his hands over his head, cradling it. His shoulders started to heave, and to the intense embarrassment of everybody, loud, wild sobs started heaving from his body, strange cries of abandonment and desolation, hopeless appeals for companionship and compassion.

'Oh my God,' he wept. 'Don't do it. Help me. Don't do it. Father. Oh my God, my God.'

# CHAPTER XIII

---

## Bass-Baritone

The rehearsal was still proceeding at five-thirty. Owen Caulfield had been taken off by Bob Whittaker, the new stage-door-keeper, and plied with coffee in one of the dressing-rooms. After observing him and listening to him for fifteen minutes Bob had phoned for an ambulance and had him taken to hospital. He came and told Mike Turner what he had done, and the news sent a frisson of fascinated, slightly guilty interest through the assembled company. But they soon got down, with a sense of relief, to rehearsing under Simon Mulley, who had been put in temporary charge by Mike. Giulia Contini's threat of withdrawal had not been acted upon, and she now seemed to have forgotten all about it. Simon praised, demonstrated, advised, and in general created a relaxed atmosphere, which meant that more useful work was done in half an hour than in five hours of Owen's uncreative tension. Even Barbara Bootle, after a little weep at her own daring and its result, started walking across the stage in a natural manner, and though she still looked more like a transport café waitress than an Italian tart, still everyone agreed it was a step in the right direction.

Superintendent Nichols had earlier had a whispered consultation with PC Lyme about the results of his foot-slogging, and had listened with interest to his impressions and deductions. He determined to interview Hurtle in the theatre and watch his reactions, and when he arrived, on the dot of five-thirty, he certainly seemed interested in what was going on on stage. He draped himself across three seats next to Nichols and watched the quartet being performed for the third time that day.

'Jeez, was that Gaylene's part?' he said. 'I think she'd have put more into it.'

'Yes, I gather her stand-in is having her problems,' said Nichols.

'Following Gaylene was always a bit of a problem,' said Hurtle, conjuring up visions of Gaylene trailing clouds of anti-climax in her wake. 'You can say what you like about the chap that did it, but he certainly had nerve!'

'Some people would say that you would be the type that had the nerve,' said Nichols, watching him closely. 'And the motive.'

'Sure they would,' said Hurtle genially. 'If I'd thought she was serious about the engagement—well, Jeez, one of us would have had to go!'

'But you didn't?'

'Think she was serious? Don't make me laugh! Only thing that worried me was, I thought she might be having difficulty finding men, because that would be the only thing that would make her actually get married. I said so to this Owen bloke, but he said "I believe not" in that stiff pommie way. That put my mind at rest. It wasn't funny thinking I might be the straw she was clutching at!'

Something clicked in Nichols's mind. Owen had professed to be ignorant as to whether Hurtle knew about Gaylene's sleeping habits. It seemed clear that Hurtle knew, and Owen knew he knew. Nichols merely said: 'You give the impression this engagement was news to you.'

'Too bloody right. But I played along for the newspapers. I thought to myself that Gaylene must have her reasons, and we Aussies stick together when we're abroad, you know.'

'You didn't envisage continuing the engagement after you left Manchester?'

'Jeez, no! I've got three nice little typists from Melbourne lined up in Cardiff. Sharing a bed-sitter. Even old Gaylene couldn't have competed with that!' He grinned in promiscuous anticipation.

'But theoretically you could have done all the attempts and the actual murders. You have no real alibi.'

'Fair enough,' said Hurtle, with unabated geniality. 'Except I was in Southampton the night she was gassed. I suppose you'll have checked on the trains?'

'Yes. It's pretty unlikely, but just possible. It wouldn't have done your game any good.'

'Scored three tries next day,' said Hurtle complacently. 'How was I supposed to get into the theatre, on the night of the actual murder?'

'There was a small window leading on to a side passage.'

'How small?' asked Hurtle, surveying his enormous bulk with considerable self-satisfaction. Nichols gave up that line of thought.

'Or you could have told Harrison you were fetching something for Miss Ffrench,' he said.

'Do you think I'm a complete nong?' said Hurtle scornfully.

Nichols paused.

'Well, no,' he said. 'Actually, I'd have said you put on a pose—of amiable dimness, if you'll excuse the expression. But that you're really rather sharp.'

Hurtle's face lit up in an enormous beam.

'Put it on for the Poms,' he said. 'We all do. They expect it.'

The rehearsal was at last nearing its end. Simon Mulley was crooning over the rotund sack in which was the body of his daughter, and Giulia Contini was floating some delicious high notes as she prepared to go and join her mother in heaven. She was at last giving some indication of how she had made her reputation. Nichols suspected that she was one of those Italians who thrived on a good blow-up row.

'That's a real nice sound,' said Hurtle, and stayed on to listen.

When it was all over, and the stage-hands prepared to dismantle the dingy Mantuan inn and erect a spick-and-span Neapolitan café for the night's Così, Nichols slipped down and had a word with Mike Turner. Mike clapped his hands, and using a volume of voice and a natural authority Nichols would not have thought him capable of he called the whole cast together and told them Nichols would like a word with them. Then he set them an example and hopped over into the stalls himself.

As the others drifted in Nichols noted the ones he knew and one or two he didn't. Bridget he recognized from the first scene; that middle-aged piece of self-effacement must surely be Mr Pettifer. The attitudes of the company as they came in were various: some showed frank interest, some bewilderment, some a concealed apprehension. Some had removed their make-up already, some were still crudely over-coloured for their parts, and Jim McKaid was already costumed and made up for the part of Don Alfonso in *Così*, and looked the elderly cynic to the life.

When they saw that Hurtle was in the theatre, one or two went over to him to express sympathy. Nichols watched in amusement. They didn't know how to do it, and Hurtle certainly didn't know how to receive it. Amiable dimness was of no help to him now. After a few moments he managed to put the subject behind him, and then he got into an animated conversation with Mike Turner and Giulia Contini. When they had all got into the stalls and were standing around in rather awkward little groups Superintendent Nichols jumped up on to the podium that Mike Turner had just vacated and cleared his throat. Like well-trained schoolchildren, everyone turned towards him and put on expressions of polite interest. No doubt they were in fact genuinely interested, but it seemed to Nichols that with theatrical people even when an emotion was felt, it had also to be assumed.

'I'd like to thank you, first of all, for your co-operation in telling us your movements on the various dates which . . . which we needed to check up on,' he said, thinking how banal everything he said sounded after the heightened passions that had just been issuing from the stage. 'All the information you've given us has been very useful.'

But it hadn't. Not very. And that was what he had to take up with them now.

'The problem is,' he said, 'that the murder and the attempts could have been set up at almost any time—in each case, there's a long period *within which* it must have been done. This means it's difficult or impossible for any of you to cover yourselves. The . . . business in Miss Ffrench's dressing-room, for example, could have been done at any time after it was vacated the night before almost up until Miss Ffrench put her hand on the door-knob. Then again, the gas-fire could have been turned on at more or less any time during the night or early morning. It's very difficult for anyone to get any sort of reliable alibi for that length of time. And in case any of you are still not taking those early attempts very seriously, I'd ask you to remember Sergeant Harrison.'

At once all the faces surrounding him in the stalls went grave in unison, again like school-children.

'That murder is a rather different kettle of fish,' said Nichols, 'because there we can fix a fairly exact time. But confining ourselves for the moment to the attempts on Miss Ffrench, and coming to this difficult question of alibis, it seems as if, almost without exception, the whole cast of *Rigoletto* who had been rehearsing with her, and who are naturally among the first we think of, could have rigged up the device whch killed her. Or, for that matter, perpetrated any of the potentially fatal attempts. This doesn't make our job any easier.'

Did he imagine it, or was there a unanimous relaxation of facial muscles? Did they not want him to find the murderer? Or perhaps they all did Gaylene in, as in that silly film his wife had dragged him along to last month.

'The only exception,' he went on, 'is Mr Ricci. As you know, on the night before Miss Ffrench's death Mr Ricci was singing in Oslo. And he didn't arrive back in Manchester until after Miss Ffrench's death. This is something we've checked with Oslo, of course, and they have confirmed that Mr Ricci did indeed sing in—' he paused, as if not quite sure how to pronounce it—'*Don Giovanni* that evening, and that he was seen off on the plane at Fornebu airport the next morning at nine by the deputy manager of the Norwegian Opera. Of course we will have to go carefully into the question of chartered planes, but that seems very unlikely, and since there is no other way Mr Ricci could have got to Manchester and then back to Oslo between the end of the performance there and being picked up by the Norwegian gentleman the next morning, I think we can say that he—and he alone of the company—is in the clear.'

The heads all looked in Raymond Ricci's direction, and there played around the edges of his lips the tiniest suspicion of a smile.

'There is only one thing that puzzles me,' said Nichols. The smile evaporated from the corners of the mouth, and Ricci expressed with his large Italian eyes a polite interest in what was to come. 'You showed me a copy of the review of your per-

formance in the Oslo *Morgenbladet*. Of course I
don't read Norwegian, and nor do you, but still I
rather gathered from puzzling over the few words
that were clear, that the writer declared that your
Giovanni was vocally in the tradition of Brownlee
and Gobbi, isn't that so?' Nichols was gratified to
see that all heads in the theatre turned towards
Ricci with a puzzled expression on their faces.
'Brownee and Gobbi rather than Pinza and Siepi,
wasn't that what the writer said? Well, actually, I
know it was, because that's another thing I've
checked up on with our opposite numbers in Oslo.
Now, I find that very puzzling, you know. Because
as of course you all know, the role of Don Giovanni
can be sung by a baritone voice or by a bass—in
fact people dispute which is the most suitable, isn't
that right?'

The heads nodded, still looking at Ricci.

'Now Pinza and Siepi are among the best-known
bass Giovannis, and Brownlee and Gobbi are or
were both baritones. And yet you, who are indis-
putably a bass as I have had the pleasure of hearing this afternoon, are classed by the critic as being
firmly in the baritone tradition. Of course I am very
much the amateur enthusiast where opera is concerned—could you tell me if I am completely off-
beam?'

# CHAPTER XIV

### *Ella Giammai M'Amo*

'THAT'S *Così Fan Tutte*. Mozart, you know.' Calvin was remembering his words to Nichols. Condescending oaf that I am, he thought. How he must have been laughing at us all, assuming he was pig-ignorant. He flushed with embarrassment as he thought: what a steam I would have got up if someone had done the same to me!

'Mozart, you know. Lovely little piece.' McKaid was remembering his words to Nichols. And all the time the cunning little bastard was an opera buff, a canary fancier. Probably an LP collector with a little padded cell to listen to his records in, or earphones to keep the children's noise out. Probably a teenage galleryite grown up—used to go to all the touring Sadler's Wells performances, and have little arguments with his friends in the interval about opera in English versus opera in the original. Underhand little shit. I'll have to change my tone to him. Geniality—'you really had us fooled there'— that sort of tone. Only thing to do in the circumstances. Not that it matters.

\* \* \*

'I'm not going to make a fool of myself by sitting here and explaining what you know already,' said Raymond Ricci, sprawling in a chair in the stage-door-keeper's office later in the evening, with the strains of *Così Fan Tutte* penetrating now and then as Bridget's voice, seeming to gain in fullness and beauty every performance, soared over the others in the big ensembles. Ricci was oblivious of the sounds, occasionally drumming his fingers and looking at Nichols with a not-entirely-confident smile.

'Not know—suspect,' said Nichols, none too friendly. 'I suspect, then, that your brother went to Oslo and sang Giovanni, and that you stayed here.' Ricci nodded. 'You relied on us not checking too closely *who* was actually singing in Oslo. In fact, I was already suspicious, and Lyme's report of your landlady's conversation made me even more so. Now—why?'

'He's a good singer. He's sung a few small parts here, and understudied some larger ones, but he's never quite got the chances he deserves. I thought I might be holding him back, overshadowing him, in a way. I don't suppose it's helped him that I'm not the most generally loved member of the company, though recently dear Gaylene has stolen my thunder there. Robert had sung Giovanni at college, and with a few semi-amateur groups, so he knew the part well. When the telegram came I decided to send him off in my place.'

'And he was able to go? Wasn't he singing?'

'No, because the chorus in *Così*, as you are no doubt aware, is very small and has hardly any part to play. He wasn't scheduled to perform that night anyway.'

'And all this was done out of pure altruism?'

There was a short silence.

'Do you know, Superintendent,' said Ricci with a saturnine smile on his face, 'if I were to tell you it was, I have a suspicion you wouldn't believe me.'

'Put it down to the cynicism of my profession,' said Nichols. 'Now let's stop fooling and have the whole story out.'

Again there was a pause.

'This isn't going to please you, Superintendent,' said Raymond Ricci at last, 'but I can't tell you what I was doing that night.'

Is he expecting me to say: oh what a pity, well never mind? thought Nichols. He raised his voice a little and looked Ricci straight in the face.

'It's not really a question of what pleases me, is it?' he said. 'Here you are, caught out in a lie to the police about your movements. Inevitably we are suspicious, and more than suspicious, since no reason for the lie suggests itself, except the murder. If you don't want us to hold you for further questioning, I would suggest it's very much in your interest to give us as full an account of yourself as possible.'

'Precisely,' said Ricci, who did not seem unduly impressed by this lecture, but whose fingers were still drumming periodically on the side of the chair. 'And that's what I'd like to do. The trouble is, I'm not the only one in question. There's somebody else to be considered. Look—the best I can do is this: I'll consult with that other person as soon as possible, and if I get the OK I'll come along with the whole story. Will that satisfy you?'

'It will not,' said Nichols. 'I'd need to be quite sure you wouldn't do a bunk on us. We'd look right fools if we'd had you and let you go on the strength of a flimsy story like that. Especially as, like the rest, you now have no alibi for any of the attempts on Miss Ffrench.'

'True,' said Ricci, with the beginnings of a triumphant smile on his face. 'But what about the murder of Sergeant Harrison? That's another matter, isn't it?'

Nichols glanced at the little card which Ricci had filled in.

'I'm afraid we've been so busy breaking down your Oslo alibi, sir,' he said suavely, 'that we haven't had the time to investigate this. I gather you were performing at some kind of concert.'

'Precisely. A musical evening for the combined C of E and Non-Conformist congregations of Accrington and Oswaldtwistle. Compered by the Mayor, no less. I suppose they invited a Catholic singer as an ecumenical gesture. Now what time was Harrison killed?'

'As far as we can make out, about five past ten. He phoned us about ten to, and promised to come in to speak to us. A bus went past his door at about ten past, and we imagine he'd try to catch that. He was found still warm by a neighbour before quarter past.'

The smile had not left Ricci's face.

'Well, then: at five minutes to ten o'clock, before a large and fairly enthusiastic audience of Accringtonians, I began to sing an aria which the chairman of the evening announced as "Ella Jemima Mo"— which made it sound like a Victorian temperance campaigner, or some such type. I hardly need tell you, with your wide knowledge of the subject, which aria he referred to.' Nichols bent his head gravely. It is, as you know, a longish aria. I noticed the time because it was the last item for the evening, and I had a train to catch. Any questions?'

'None. If you were singing any time after about a quarter past nine you more or less must be in the clear. I presume the Mayor or someone else who was there could vouch for this.'

'No doubt,' said Ricci confidently. 'Do go ahead and check.'

Nichols took up the phone and barked orders. In a couple of minutes he was through and putting his question.

'So he was singing about ten? . . . Yes, a long aria, that's it . . . Yes, I'm sure he sang it nicely, but I wonder if you could describe him . . . Yes—him personally—what he looks like . . . Yes, it sounds like him, but then, it could equally well be his brother . . . Oh, you've seen his brother? . . . He was performing as well, I see . . . Duets . . . Yes, well, I'll send a photograph just to be sure, but I think that puts Mr Ricci in the clear . . . I'm most grateful for your help, sir.'

And making the ritual noises that local big-wigs take for granted as one of the perks of office, Nichols put the phone down and turned towards an annoyingly complacent Ricci.

'Looks as if you're in the clear,' he said. 'For the Harrison murder anyway.'

'I can't say I blame you for not trusting me,' said Ricci, his fingers now completely still. 'But I assure you you'll find that I *was* singing at that concert.'

'You seem to assume,' said Nichols with pardonable sourness, 'that because you are in the clear for the Harrison murder, you are in the clear all around.'

'Not at all," said Ricci. 'I'm just asking you to take the chance you just now said you were unwilling to take. *Because* I'm in the clear for Harrison, and *because* the same person probably did both, the risk is less than you made out. *Therefore* it's worth giving me a few hours to clear my story, and then hopefully, as the Americans say, I'll be back to lay it on the line, go the hang-out road.'

His voice had taken on an American twang, and his face had assumed a comically furtive, Nixonian expression. Nichols didn't much like his over-confidence, because, like all policemen, he objected to being lied to. Still, leaving aside the fact that he didn't greatly like this young man, what he said made a kind of sense.

'OK,' he said wearily. 'You can go. But I shall want to see you tomorrow morning, before eleven if you please. And I shall want the story to be good.'

'Good I cannot promise you,' said Raymond Ricci, 'but interesting—probably.'

'I still don't trust him,' said Sergeant Chappell, as he went out.

'He seems to go out of his way *not* to be trusted,' said Nichols. 'These people are rather like children in a lot of ways—no one wants to be the good boy in the class.'

'The devil of it is,' said Chappell, 'if he is in the clear we are pretty much back to square one.'

'Exactly. A lot of singers with no alibis, one or two with dicey alibis for one or other of the attempts which are pure hell to check and probably hold very little water, and no lead towards a motive except general and freely admitted dislike. It's a hell of a small haul after four days' work.'

'What will the next step be, then?'

'I suppose we dig into the background of all the more important people who have been around Gaylene Ffrench for these past few weeks. And failing that, into the recent career of the girl herself, which should be a jolly task for someone or other. If she hasn't made life-long enemies in every single city she's sung in since she came to these shores, I'm no judge of character. Then there are these various slanders against one or other of the cast—the slanders which Ricci repeated so readily. We'll have to look especially hard at those, I suppose, but really we need to dig deeply into *everyone's* background, and that will be pure slog.'

'I wonder if the girl had any friends,' said Chappell, 'not sleeping partners, which is all we've dug up here, but the sort of girl-friend she might really natter away to.'

Nichols contemplated the suggestion with some contempt.

'Have you ever known a girl like that have friends of her own sex?' he asked. 'Any other woman would reach for her hat-pin at the mere sight of her. As for nattering—well, we haven't lacked for a natter so far, have we? And has there been anything in it to go on? We could have done with a good deal less nattering, in my opinion, and a good deal more hard, observed fact.'

Sergeant Chappell looked depressed. 'I wonder if she said anything in her letters home,' he said.

'"Dear Mum and Dad, had a fabulous success last week. Please send large jar of vegemite, love Gaylene." All right—it's something we could look into, but if our Miss Ffrench was the writing home type, I'll eat my police medal.' He got up. 'Well, I suppose that's it for the night. Tomorrow morning I think I'll have a word with this man Mulley. We've no particular reason to think that he and Gaylene ever crossed swords, but he looked an interesting type. Bigamy was his particular little secret, wasn't it, according to Gaylene? That's a real, nice, old-fashioned crime, like breach of promise, or conspiracy to publish an obscene article. I don't see murder being committed to hide it, though, do you? With the sleeping habits of these people we should be so pleased if any of them consent to get married at all that we ought to turn a blind eye if they decide to do it twice.'

Outside the stage-door-keeper's office he heard the sounds of a theatre closing down for the night. He heard Bob whistling in the distance, and saw Bridget Lander departing after what he guessed was another clamorously received performance. He must try to talk to her tomorrow too, but he hoped against hope she had nothing to do with it: he hadn't yet had time to see her Fiordiligi himself.

He was about to turn out into the street when his departure was arrested by an apparition, an incongruous vision. The stage-door opened, and there floated through it a stunning woman: a woman of great natural beauty and some unobtrusively applied beauties, a woman whose rose-pink freshness not even the grime of late-night Manchester could sully, a woman whose simple, striking clothes seemed to bear a tiny label saying 'outrageously expensive'. But overpowering all these impressions was one of sheer femininity, the sort of femininity which began going out of fashion with the silent screen, and received its death-blow with the onrush of militancy in the sixties. This was a woman of charm, ambiguous attractions, tantalizing promise, unspoken invitation. This was a woman who knew exactly what she wanted, and would get it.

Who on earth was she? Nichols asked himself. Not, he felt sure, an opera-singer. None but the most lavishly overpaid could afford to dress like that, and none of the three or four current idols of the galleryites and micro-groove fanatics looked like that. Not remotely like that.

She was about to pass him when she pulled herself up short, with great grace, and fixed him with the sort of ravishing smile that sent men off to die happy in the trenches, and might have doomed the bachelorhood of Sherlock Holmes himself.

'Superintendent Nichols?' she said with an enchanting query in her Fenella Fielding voice. 'My husband has told me about you. Are you any further forward with this awful business of that poor girl?'

Husband? What husband? thought Nichols to himself. Paul Getty Jnr? A minor Rockefeller? One of the Bay City Rollers?

'Not too far forward, I'm afraid,' he said, with one of the cagily ingratiating smiles policemen keep for monied nobs with a tendency to interfere.

'It's one of those amorphous cases where even the times are difficult to pin down, let alone anything else.'

'I gathered from the little Michael told me . . .' began the vision.

Michael. Must be Mike Turner's wife, thought Nichols. And then, irreverently: Christ, he managed to land himself a world-beater. His emotion, most uncharacteristically, must have surfaced on to his face, because the vision noticed it and pulled herself up.

'Maddening of me not to have introduced myself—do forgive me,' she said. 'Cecily Turner—though I'm afraid most people still think of me as Cecily Dobber.'

The voice sank with husky insinuation. Dobber. Unusual name. Was she bringing it to his notice with some ulterior purpose? Suddenly the name rang a tiny bell inside Nichols's brain, and the ex-Miss Dobber seemed to hear it ring.

'Exactly,' she said, with a deprecating smile. 'Dobberware. I'm afraid my father invented it, and made unconscionable amounts of money out of it. Sets of little plastic bowls and boxes and pots and saucers and goodness knows what—though *what* people found to do with them, I've never quite discovered.'

Dobberware, thought Nichols—the foundation for the Turner smoothness. Once again the splendid creature seemed to follow his thoughts, and leap ahead of him.

'Quite,' she said with a dazzling smile. 'Hence this.' She gave a graceful wave of the hand which seemed to imply the opera company as a whole.

'Or part of it. Rather a larger part, it sometimes seems to me, than . . .' She paused for a second in mid-sentence, and then said: 'I mean, of course, that I'm not *quite* sure whether I intended to marry an opera company when I married Mike. But I suppose you can say it has given him a plaything, and me an excuse for leave of absence—*anywhere* rather than this terrible city—not even the most unreasonable husband could have expected it. Certainly Michael didn't. Which is why I never met the poor girl herself . . .'

Nichols's mind had been travelling exotically, visualizing this creature in Cannes, in Tangiers, in African big-game reserves. He realized with a start that she was again talking about Gaylene. She seemed to be leading up to something, and as usual she got there disconcertingly quickly.

'I suppose you couldn't say whether Mike and she had been sleeping together, could you?' she said.

He was so taken off his guard that he nearly behaved unprofessionally. After a pause he cleared his throat. 'I'm afraid that's something I . . .'

'No, of course you couldn't. Foolish of me to ask it, wasn't it? But it would have made things so much simpler.'

At that moment Bob appeared down the dusty corridor, about his late-night business. Mrs Turner flashed in his direction a smile which seemed to leave him groggily uncertain whether to tug his forelock or wilt at the knees. He smiled feebly and took to his heels. Cecily Turner apparently decided it was time to be going.

'I mustn't keep you,' she said, in a voice that

Nichols could have sworn was leading up to something. 'Silly of me to have prattled on like this when you have so much to do.' She floated a few steps along the corridor, and then turned with a smile which had clearly been under preparation while her back was towards him—a smile of great subtlety and insinuation.

'Tell me, Superintendent,' she said, fluting her voice across the distance between them with no attempt at concealment or confidentiality at all, 'if I were to find my financial affairs were . . . not quite as I expected them to be, and if it turned out not to be a matter for an accountant, but for the police, would you, I wonder, would you allow me to come with my little troubles to you?'

'I should be del . . .'

'Too kind,' cooed Cecily Turner. 'Really terribly kind. I have had so little experience of anything of that sort . . . Hitherto . . .'

And with a 'Goodbye' that held acres of wistfulness and promise, she resumed her forward progress. Nichols felt he had to steady himself by the doorpost a moment to cushion the after-effects of her impact. When rationality and scepticism regained some foothold in his mind, it occurred to him that his part in the conversation had hardly amounted to more than a dozen words. It also occurred to him that he was being used. An interesting experience, and by no means an unpleasant one. But still, as a policeman he felt he had to know: used for what?

Another thought came to him, and this time an unworthy one: if Mrs Turner of the plastic pots

was going to visit Mr Turner of the opera company, would they talk about? And—more to the
point—where would they talk about it? In view of
the personal nature of the conversation she had
just had with him, a complete stranger, in the corridor of a theatre, it did not seem as if privacy were
one of Cecily Turner's aims. He lit a cigarette, with
the conscious aim of giving the Turners time to
get together and stuck into whatever subject was
closest to the gorgeous Cecily's heart. If she had
taken the trouble to come to the theatre after the
performance, it was to be presumed that they
wouldn't go home to have it out.

After he had puffed his way through a third of
his Player's he decided he was strong enough to
resist the divine Cecily's charms, particularly if
they were directed against somebody else. He set
off down the corridor, his nostrils twitching to dis-
cover the direction taken by a subtle perfume
which had environed Mrs Turner—a perfume, no
doubt, with a sensual name and an unearthly price.
Finally the murmur of voices from the stalls convinced him he had reached his goal. He made his
way to the main exit at the back—where, he had
previously noticed, there were double swinging
doors which opened and shut quite noiselessly. He
tested them out, and stood quite quiet behind
heavy curtains, now and then peeping through to
see the two people in the body of the murky theatre. Mike had been conducting earlier in the evening, and had probably come back for his score.
He was still in tails, and he had obviously just descended from the podium in order to confront at

closer quarters his wife, who was draped over a seat in the front row. Together they looked like something out of Noel Coward or early Waugh.

'But why?' Mike was saying. 'Why now? Everything's been going all right, hasn't it?'

'As far as I can see,' drawled Cecily, 'nothing much has been going at all. Not that you are particularly to blame for that, and I won't deny it has suited me. You've been going your way, I've been going mine—just as we said. We've had a business arrangement, haven't we, rather than a marriage. Well, the fact is, darling, it's become a bit of a bore having a husband and *not* having a husband. It gives you all the disadvantages of respectability with none of the advantages. And the fact is, I want to get married—really married this time.'

'In other words, you don't just want a divorce, you want a quick, easy divorce.'

'Precisely. You know I believe in keeping men waiting just so long and no longer. I don't intend to let my little lordling get tired of waiting for me.'

'Aha—it's a title you're after, is it?'

Cecily shrugged her shapely shoulders. 'Not *exactly*, darling. I mean, not any old title. I wouldn't fall over backwards for one of Mr Wilson's life peers, for example. Even daddy refused one of those. But this is an awfully *good* title—I mean old, and hereditary—lots of money and land, and a family that's been perfectly useless and undistinguished for generations. That sort of thing does rather attract a woman, you know. Such a piquant contrast to the Dobberware!'

'And you expect me to provide evidence of "irretrievable breakdown" or whatever they call it so that you can take up your position as a lady of the manor, serving nourishing soup to the poor in Dobberware bowls?'

'Precisely, dear. Bouillabaisse, I think, with coq au vin to follow. No point in stinting things. And by the way, it's rather more than a manor. The point really is, my dear Michael, that the courts won't need much evidence. We've hardly been together for more than four or five weeks in the past eighteen months. And I've no doubt at all that you've been amusing yourself now and then on the side, though I've never till now been interested enough to want to know for certain.'

There was a pause. 'There has been no one,' said Mike.

'Oh come, darling,' cooed Cecily. 'Utter celibacy? I know you better than that.'

'No one,' repeated Mike.

'Do I detect,' said Cecily, still perfectly dovelike but with a few traces of Noel Coward's Amanda showing through her poise, 'do I detect signs of non-co-operation? A digging in of the heels?'

'Call it that if you like. I'm damned if I'm going to let the marriage tail off without we make some attempt to make a go of it. For a start all this—' he gestured round the grubby plush and gilt of the Prince of Wales Theatre—'collapses round my ears.'

'I thought that's what would worry you most,' said Cecily. 'And I'd be willing to continue a small grant, annually. Now someone who is as near tonedeaf as makes no difference couldn't say fairer than that, could she?'

Nichols, peeping through the curtains, noted

there was one man who was completely impervious to Cecily's charms.

'A small grant,' Mike said impatiently. 'What do you think a small grant buys these days? A few bangles for Carmen and a couple of pillars for Sarastro's temple. Thanks for nothing.'

Mike's voice was getting desperate, but Cecily seemed to have no trouble at all in keeping her beautifully articulated cool.

'I think you'll find I have a better idea than you imagined as to how far money goes these days. In fact, you've been finding that even a quite generous grant doesn't go as far as you thought, haven't you? I know perfectly well, my dear Michael, that one can't run an eight-month opera season on the pittance you got from the Arts Council last year and the sum we agreed on together.'

There was silence in the theatre. Then Cecily's voice came clear and cold—a voice with money in it, not the money that buys luxury, but the money that buys power.

'Unless you do as I ask, the accountants will be looking into my financial affairs by the weekend, and the police will be brought in by Monday. Do I make myself clear?'

# CHAPTER XV

---

*Recapitulation*

'Do you think we should go and see Owen?' said Calvin to Bridget, as he watched her dress and make up for the final dress-rehearsal, and wished she, rather than the unexciting Giulia Contini, were playing Gilda. Bridget peered closely at her face in the mirror, then expertly pencilled over her eyebrows.

'Why?' she said.

'Well,' said Calvin, and hesitated, because there was no very obvious reason except pity, 'it seems tough on him—being sacked after all those rehearsals, and then breaking down in front of all of us.'

'But what makes you think he would want to see us?' asked Bridget, attacking an eyelash and blinking experimentally.

'Well—' again Calvin was irresolute, 'it's just that Owen hadn't many friends . . .'

'True. And we certainly weren't among them,' said Bridget. 'The fact is that he hadn't many friends—or to be more exact he hadn't any friends—because he didn't want friends. I suppose you think I'm being hard?'

'Yes, I do rather.'

'Well, if it will make you feel any better, go and ring the hospital and see if there's any point in our going. There's no reason to get steamed up about it before we know that.'

Calvin, still vaguely unhappy, went out, leaving Bridget gingerly trying on her wig. As he went down the corridor on the way to the phone he passed Nichols, and was surprised to see the stolid, capable-looking policeman start at the sight of him. Then he remembered he was already 'whited up' for the part of the Duke of Mantua. A bitter quip at Nichols's expense rose to his mind, but after relishing it for a second, he put it aside: the last time he had tried to put the Superintendent into a stereotyped mould, he had leapt rather spectacularly out of it. And he must look odd, with his deadly white colouring and negroid lips. Not so odd as some Otellos, though, he told himself.

He put his money into the pay phone near the stage door that company members were supposed to use. The hospital was efficient and sympathetic, but not very hopeful.

'For the moment, sir, we feel there wouldn't be much point in encouraging visitors. There has been family come, of course, but he doesn't recognize anybody. If you'd like to ring in a day or two, we can tell you then whether or not there's any change.'

Calvin put the phone down. He was sorry to find that he was glad that he need not see Owen. He told himself it would be better for all concerned if they went to visit him after the first night.

*    *    *

Raymond Ricci was pleased with himself. Very obviously pleased with himself. His lips were itching to smile in triumph, and his eyes sparkled with self-satisfaction.

'Right, then,' he said to Nichols and Chappell, once again sitting in their armchair, but this time entirely at his ease. 'Here are the details. I was sleeping with Giulia Contini.'

'Yes,' said Nichols, 'I thought it would have something to do with sleeping.'

'She's staying at the Metropole. I went to her room at ten—skulked would be a better description, I think. Playing Sparafucile you get very good at skulking. Anyway, I was in her bedroom with her all night, and about six forty-five I skulked out again.'

'I see, sir. And Miss Contini will be willing to confirm your statement, will she?'

'Perfectly.'

'I don't quite understand all the secrecy and skulking, and the pretending to go to Oslo. You don't usually seem to feel the need to cover up your activities in this way.'

'No—well, the problem, you see, was Signor Pratelli. He seems to see himself as a sort of Horatius keeping the bridge of Giulia's virtue. I gather he's sworn an oath by the nine gods to Giulia's parents that their daughter shall remain pure and spotless even though her career takes her to flashy vice-spots such as Manchester. He's like an eighteenth-century duenna, only even more unattractive and snuffly. So you see, we decided that if we were going to get married—'

'Married?'

'Yes, married, Superintendent—if we were going to get married, we ought to sort of try things out first, and to do that we had to put old Pratelli off the scent first. He'd marked me down as a lady-killer, I don't know why.' Smirk. 'So he was on his guard against me, and though we snatched a few meetings here and there, he kept his beady little eyes trained on me, and mostly spotted me coming a mile off. Then when I announced that I was on my way to Oslo, he relaxed.'

'And then . . .'

'Then Giulia said to him that she had to go to bed early on account of the dress rehearsal the next day, then I popped in to the hotel, and hey, as they say, presto.'

There was a moment's silence.

'Of course your personal affairs are nothing to do with me,' said Nichols, 'but isn't marriage rather a new départure for you, sir?'

'Rather,' said Raymond Ricci with a lazy smile. 'But we Italians always come to it in the end, you know. And when we do, we prefer the homely type to the sex-kittens—we keep them as side-dishes. Now that's exactly what Giulia is—a nice, comfortable girl. And when she's sung herself out—say four or five years, because her reputation is inflated already, and won't stand the breath of international competition—we'll settle down on the proceeds, and raise a lot of little Riccis. And all the boys will have splendid bass-baritone voices, and they'll be able to interchange as Don Giovanni.'

'I see,' said Nichols, who did all too well. Giulia

was destined for a life of domestic slavery. 'So Miss Contini can vouch for you all night—not that it matters.'

'Well, she slept a bit, naturally.'

'The point's not vital. You could have fixed up the electrocution in the early morning.'

'True. I didn't, but true.'

'At any rate, that's all I need to know for the moment. I suppose I should wish you every happiness, sir.'

If Nichols had been a theatrical person, he would have spoken that last sentence through his teeth. But Ricci did not appear to notice the reluctance of his benevolent hopes.

'A bit premature, as yet,' he said airily. 'Nothing's final, you know. When it is, dear old Pratelli will get the push, and things'll be a whole lot easier.'

Ricci got up. 'And that, then,' he said, 'is the story of how my little brother got his big chance. All For Love, or Oslo well lost.'

'I still don't like that smarmy bugger,' said Chappell as he closed the door.

'Not my idea of the perfect lover either,' said Nichols.

Simon Mulley was late preparing for the final dress rehearsal, and would infinitely have preferred not talking to Nichols at all. But finally he sat down in the corner of his dressing-room and let him ask away as he prepared himself for the performance. In his everyday clothes Simon Mulley was a good-looking middle-aged man, whose sad eyes oddly contradicted the touch of dandyism in his dress. In his costume, even Rigoletto's jester's costume,

he took on an air of utter seriousness and dedica-
tion. His manner was reasonable, courteous in a
rather old-fashioned way, but there were moments
when Nichols caught a glimpse of the iron determi-
nation, of the rigid artistic standards which made
it so difficult for him to compromise and which had
meant a career infinitely less full of plushy acclaim
and inflated fees than those of many less gifted
contemporaries.

'You mustn't think of this as an unpleasant or
unfriendly company to work with, full of rows and
ructions,' he said, smoothing down the ruff around
his scarlet costume, and looking at himself critical-
ly in the mirror. 'It's probably sounded like that to
you, but of course all you've been interested in has
been the things that have happened since Gaylene
Ffrench's arrival.'

'Certainly I seem to have been hearing about an
awful lot of nastiness and petty spite,' said Nichols.

'I guessed you would have. But in point of fact
we'd been an exceptionally united and serious little
company until she arrived. In fact, we'd had the
sort of unflashy, hard-working spirit that you don't
often get in opera houses. Until she came, there
was nobody in the company who was trying to
push himself forward, and in fact everybody—or
nearly everybody, because I'm not saying things
were perfection—nearly everybody was trying to
get a good *company* performance. I was reminded
of Sadler's Wells in the old Tucker days, when I
was a young man. I sang some performances of
*Tosca* for Turner last season in Liverpool, and I
was so impressed I agreed at once to join as a
regular company member for this season. I'm doing

Rigoletto now, and there are some Papagenos and some di Lunas coming up later in the season. It's just been sad from my point of view that the atmosphere so far has been so different from what it was earlier.'

'You've regretted agreeing to join the company?'

'Regretted? I don't know about that. One shouldn't make up one's mind too hastily—I've made enough bad snap decisions in my time to be sure of that. But certainly this Gaylene Ffrench was a poisonous influence, a real thug. And her influence spread wider and wider. Caulfield, the producer—well, he's not a stable type at the best of times I'd guess, but these last few weeks he has seemed to get tenser and tenser. Cross, who's got real talent and feeling for opera—she could put him off his stride by a flick of the eyelid. Oh yes, it's not the same company as it was last year. Though luckily we seem to be getting back to normal now, as far as that's possible with a murder investigation going on around one.'

'You didn't have any brushes with Miss Ffrench yourself?'

'Oh no.' Simon Mulley smiled. He had made up his face and it was now the face of a bitter, worn elderly man, so the smile came out bitterly, but Nichols had the odd impression of seeing two different faces at once, and he thought the smile underneath the make-up was comparatively untroubled. Simon went on: 'Occasionally I used my position as distinguished senior company member to put her in her place. But I fear it didn't work. Respect for position, or age, or incapacity, or anything like that wouldn't stop that miss saying something if she wanted to say it. She was the complete child of nature, untouched by any of the finer feelings of the civilized. It made one think that children of nature have been much over-rated. Anyway, when I tried to rebuke her, it fell abysmally flat, because she was far too stupid to understand.'

'You didn't sleep with her?' asked Nichols.

'Good God, no. I'd rather have slept with a sperm whale.'

Simon was sitting back in his chair to take a longer view of his make-up, and he certainly gave no indication that Nichols's question had ruffled his gentlemanly composure.

'I see,' said Nichols. 'On the other hand, Miss Ffrench seemed interested in *your* personal life, sir.'

'Really?' For the first time a note of tension seemed to enter Simon Mulley's voice. 'How is that?'

'She apparently told one of her bed-partners that you were a bigamist.'

There was a long pause. Simon finished looking at his make-up and wig, and reached round to the armchair. He took up a hard, pointed lump with a series of straps attached. Deliberately he pushed it up the back of his jester's costume, and began pulling the straps carefully over his shoulders.

'I suppose I might have guessed she would get hold of that story,' he said finally. 'And get it wrong.'

Nichols didn't hurry him, and when Mulley finally turned round to tell him the story, his hump was in position, and he had only to pick up his stick with bells on the end to be the complete Rigoletto.

Again Nichols had the odd sensation of seeing two men, related but separate.

'A long time ago,' Simon Mulley said sadly, gazing at the floor, but still carrying with him that touch of theatricality which was perhaps second nature, 'when I was much younger, but still old enough to know better, I decided to leave my wife. For no better reason than that it was the end of the season, and I thought I was in love with a little girl in the theatre ballet: she was a slip of a thing, lovely, very silly, and only nineteen. I left a note for Margaret, in the classic fashion, and we got into the car one morning, and drove to Scotland.'

He paused, and absent-mindedly adjusted his hump.

'We never got there. We were fooling around in the front seat when a truck rammed us from behind. I had concussion, and a lot of cuts and bruises . . . and a burden for life. She . . . the slip . . . had severe brain damage. A hopeless case. Since then she's never been anything more than a vegetable. She had no close family who were in a position to look after her. So I did. We did.'

'Your wife and you?'

'My wife and I. Margaret was so good it . . . shames me . . . pains me to think about it. The burden has been more on her than on me, because she has it every hour of the day, whereas I can put it out of my mind . . . nearly. When I think of it, of her, I . . . loathe myself.'

'So she lives with you?'

'Yes, she always has done, since—'

'And yet the story is more or less secret?'

'Secret? Well, it's not exactly that. I imagine people gossip about it readily enough, in London. But we've only recently taken a house up here, and most of the company is new-ish. It may be that someone had heard a whisper, and the story has grown in the telling—or someone has just got it wrong. Probably Gaylene heard of it during one of her guest appearances with one or other of the companies. I expect she either twisted it deliberately, or quite likely just got it fouled up in her mind, because as I say she was none too bright.'

'It seems likely, I admit,' said Nichols.

'And now,' said Mulley, his face twisting into a smile which seemed to bring together his own self and Rigoletto's, a smile of utter self-loathing, of hatred of all the world, 'now, I've bared my soul enough. I can only hope you've managed to put me in the mood for my role. Good afternoon, Superintendent.'

Only a theatrical person could dismiss a superintendent in such a grand manner. The upper classes had lost the knack long ago. Nichols went quietly.

The opening chords of *Rigoletto* were sounding from the orchestra pit for the final dress rehearsal as Nichols and Chappell let themselves into their little office, and depressedly surveyed the collection of junky lost property and the mess of paper and alibi cards that were the evidences of their own days of investigation. It didn't add to the attractions of the scene that they seemed likely to be settled in there for a long time to come. Because he didn't want to talk about that Nichols let the door stand open a little and nodded in time to the music. But after a bit he dragged himself over to his untidy desk and sat down, looking all too obviously depressed.

'Okay, let's talk this thing over and try and get some order into our thoughts,' he said.

Sergeant Chappell was immensely flattered by the 'our', but he didn't presume on it: he sat waiting expectantly.

'Right. We have four attempts,' said Nichols slowly, 'two of them successful. Practically any of them could have wanted to do the girl in, and in fact they all of them admit to feelings ranging from relief to pure pleasure that she has been got out of the way. On the other hand, we have no motive so far stronger than a generalized dislike. Right?'

'Right.'

'Now, while we're on the subject of motive, it's as well to be clear that there are one or two screwballs in the company, notably Owen Caulfield, who seems to have just gone over the edge, for some reason we don't know or for no reason at all. There are also one or two suspicious things going on—notably Mr Turner and his relationship to his wife's money, though what connection that could have with Gaylene God alone knows, except that knowing her she could have got wind and begun broadcasting the fact. And then, lastly, and unprofessionally, there are one or two people we two don't happen to like—notably Mr Ricci, Mr Caulfield, again, and Mr McKaid. Are you with me so far?'

'Yes.'

'And a very short distance it is too. So we come back to the attempts on Gaylene Ffrench's life. All the cast decided they were faked by the girl herself, probably for publicity purposes, though they all agree that at first she convinced them and they took her seriously. As far as we're concerned the likelihood is that all four attempts were done by the same person. On the other hand, we ought to keep in mind the possibility that the first two attempts were faked by Gaylene, and that someone took advantage of them—or was given the idea by them, which would be pretty ironic—and made a more serious attempt. The idea that the first attempts were fake is given a bit of colouring, perhaps, by the fact that though Miss Ffrench scurried along to the newspaper offices, she made no attempt to contact the police.'

'And I suppose it's just possible,' said Chappell, 'that someone did the first two as jokes, pretty nasty ones, and then someone *else* capitalized on the idea and took it for real.'

'True. Perhaps it doesn't matter too much either way. We're looking for the chappie who did the second two attempts, not the first two. But some explanation along those lines might explain the rather odd progression in the attempts.'

'Do you mean the fact that they get more and more serious as they go along?'

'Something of the kind, but I'd prefer to put it another way. The first two attempts are really rather childish. The gassing one could just have worked, but it was much more likely just to give the two of them a pretty nasty morning after the night before. But the thread on the stairs really can't be taken seriously for a moment. No one really expects to kill anybody that way, outside books, and you certainly wouldn't put an end to a healthy, bouncing girl like Gaylene Ffrench with a piece of cotton and a couple of drawing pins.

'That's true,' said Chappell. 'Either it was Gaylene, or a pretty childish mind thought that one up, you'd think. Then you come to the other two, and suddenly it's for real.'

'Yes, that how I see it. With the third attempt as somehow transitional. It was quite likely to kill her, and all the conditions were right—the hot day, the doormat, and so on. But still, he could hardly be sure. She might have smelt a rat at the doormat. She might just have been shocked—incapacitated for a bit, but not actually killed. Would he have been satisfied with that? It suggests some psycho who is just out to harm, but doesn't mind if he kills. Then you come to Harrison, where we guess the murderer felt threatened by something or other the man knew, and in that case he acts as swiftly and ruthlessly as you like.'

Chappell thought for a bit. 'You mean it's not so much a progression, a chap gaining confidence as he goes along, but more like two or three different minds at work.'

'In a way, but that seems absurd. This may not have been as nice a little company before Gaylene arrived on the scene as Mulley would like to make out, but it's stretching belief to think there could have been two or three different murderers lurking in it. It seems much more likely to be one chap gaining confidence, as you said, and then—in the Harrison case—feeling threatened and *having* to act quickly. The trouble is, I just can't see the man who wielded that mean little knife, also fiddling with little bits of thread on a dark stairway.'

'Then of course,' said Chappell, 'if we're going through possibilities, there's also the one that the two murders have no connection at all.'

'Granted. Though that would surely be stretching possibilities a bit far, wouldn't it? The point about Harrison is that he's the person most likely to have seen something suspicious on the night before Gaylene copped her packet—and the person most likely to register its significance, because there were no flies on Harrison by the sound of it: he'd been around and seen it all. If only Bob had been around that night one might have hoped to dredge something up from his memory about things he saw but didn't really register.'

'Sounds a forlorn hope.'

'Forlorn's the word for it. I'm afraid all we can do now is to dig—into everyone's background, into Gaylene's murky past, and so on. Sheer slog, but I don't see any alternative. The only thing to be done now is to get confirmation of Ricci's story. Then we'll start the whole tedious process.'

They left the office and Nichols turned to lock it up. From the direction of the stage came the sound of Giulia Contini finishing her account of 'Caro nome'.

'That girl can no more trill than a constipated owl,' said Nichols, an expression of great disgust spreading over his face.

Chappell kept quiet, because it sounded very nice to him.

# CHAPTER XVI

*Repetiteur*

When Nichols got round to the back-stage area, Giulia Contini was putting her hair in order after the token resistance she had put up, as Gilda, to her kidnapping by Jim McKaid and the male chorus. Signor Pratelli was fussing around her, like a bitch whose puppy has just taken its first steps outside the maternal basket. Nichols raised an eyebrow in her direction, and over Signor Pratelli's head Giulia nodded. Nichols went over to Calvin and Bridget and engaged them in ostentatious conversation, which set the rest of the company whispering about 'new developments'. Out of the corner of his eye he caught a glimpse of Mike Turner hurrying by, looking tense and worried. Nichols took a bet with himself that a lot of telephone conversations were taking place between him and the Arts Council in London. After a few minutes he saw Giulia Contini getting rid of Signor Pratelli, dispatching him to the stalls to report on the effect made by her entrance in the second act—not, presumably, on the effectiveness of her acting, which was still a matter of left hand, right hand, but on that perennial matter of concern to singers, whether the placing of the others on stage made it possible for her to be seen properly by all sections of the audience. As the unlikely duenna bustled off, glad to be of use, Nichols went over and took Giulia aside.

'*Grazie*,' she said. 'Is better we talks alone.'

'This won't take long,' said Nichols. 'But I'm afraid it's a little . . . embarrassing, what I have to ask you about.'

'Not is to me,' said Giulia serenely.

'Good,' said Nichols, realizing that it was himself who was embarrassed. 'Good. Yes, well, I gather that on the night before Miss Ffrench was killed, you and Mr Ricci were sleeping together at the Metropole Hotel, is that right?'

'Yes, is right.'

'And as far as you know, he was there with you all night?'

'Yes, I sink so. I not sleep so good. Is dirty, noisy city. Is like Torino, but more dirtier. So I sleep—how you say?—on and off.'

'And he left early in the morning?'

'Yes. In case old Pratelli knock on my door. 'E think 'e protecta my virtue! Ha! Is big joke—but I promise my father, is very old-fashioned, votes for Christian Democrats, and it makes 'im 'appy, so I keep Pratelli with me for a little.'

'I gather you and Mr Ricci will be getting married before very long,' said Nichols. Giulia's reaction was a wonderfully effective slow raising of the eyebrows, and then a twisting of the mouth into an expression of great contempt.

'Ha! 'E think so? Is 'nother big joke.'

'You're not intending to?'

' 'E talk of marriage. I listens and smiles and says

nothing. 'E think I not sleep with him else. 'E think Italian girls is behind the times, back in Middle Ages. 'E 'ears it from Mama and Papa, who left years and years ago. But we liberates ourselves, we Italian girls, not listens to priests and Popes no longer. We 'ave divorces and pills, and soon we all 'ave abortions. 'E not understand. 'E get a nasty surprise, that Ricci.'

'I'm sure he'll be very disappointed,' said Nichols.

'*Si, si.* 'E want to be manager mine a few years, get roles with big companies for 'imself. Then, after, 'e want mama for children, good Italian cook, 'ome-made pasta, everything! *Dio mio!* Is too pleased with 'imself, that one. I not wash 'is socks! *Brutta sorte!*'

The interview with Giulia left Nichols feeling a lot better. He hoped he would be around to witness Ricci's discomfiture. As he turned to go, he heard from the orchestral pit the beginning of the second act, and, drawn as by a magnet, he signalled to Chappell to go around front of stage. It was an act of pure self-indulgence. He had never seen a final dress rehearsal before, and during all the earlier rehearsals he had been distracted by the annoying business of having to ask people questions. Now he wanted to see properly the singers whose odd and sometimes unattractive personalities had been paraded before him in the last few days in his professional capacity.

When he and Chappell got to the stalls Calvin was beginning his aria '*Parmi veder le lagrime*', turning it, and its cabaletta, with a wonderful grace which won Nichols's whole-hearted approval: not an international star in the making, perhaps, but a tenor to be reckoned with in a world that not long ago seemed to have stopped making them. Rigoletto's distress at the loss of his daughter and his taunting by the courtiers he had seen before, but now Simon Mulley seemed to have gained in assurance, and beneath the venom and contempt one sensed a warmer, more sensitive heart: the two sides had come together, and had made a complete Rigoletto.

Signor Pratelli, sitting in the middle of the stalls, had up to this point been immobile and, Nichols suspected, as near asleep as made no difference. As the moment for his protégée's entrance approached, he automatically perked up, and began noting the placing of the various courtiers. When at last she bustled on stage, her dress minimally disarranged so as to suggest a genteel rape, her steps marginally speeded up from the usual girlish tripping to suggest her distress at this development, Signor Pratelli made several irritable gestures with his hands, called upon his God in all His three manifestations, and bustled back stage to be ready for Mike Turner at the end of the act and to make clear to him that there were certain changes in the positioning of the chorus which his Star would imperatively require.

Watching for the second time Giulia Contini's confident display of her tiny dramatic vocabulary, Nichols thought he had probably spent as much time as he could justify to himself. Turning out of his seat, and gesturing to Sergeant Chappell to follow he began tip-toeing out towards the back of the stalls. Only then did he notice the dim figure of Mr Pettifer the repetiteur, sitting in the back stalls and noting the results of his endeavours. As he approached him up the gangway Nichols, on an impulse, stopped and said: 'She'll never be an actress, that one.'

Mr Pettifer shook his head sadly. 'I think they save all their drama for life, the Italians,' he said. 'They seem to droop, emotionally, the moment they set foot on stage.'

Something of intelligence and sharp observation in Mr Pettifer's remark made Nichols linger with him. His name had come up now and again in the various conversations he had had with members of the cast, but he had not thought it worth while hitherto to interview him, because there had been no question of his crossing swords with Gaylene, certainly none of his having slept with her, and the general impression given—augmented by the appearance of the man, when he caught the occasional glimpse of him—was of someone notable only for utter inconspicuousness. It now occurred to him to wonder whether he might not be one of those whose very inconspicuousness made them the ideal observer. He also wondered how many wearing years of singers' tantrums and conductors' whims had been needed to batter the man into near-total anonymity.

'At least the acting is something you don't have to feel responsible for yourself,' Nichols said to him pleasantly.

'No, indeed,' said Mr Pettifer. He leant forward, his droopy little moustache seeming to twitch with amused irritation. 'But listen to the words! Or rather the vowels. There one could do absolutely nothing. She might as well be singing in Swahili.'

Nichols nodded sympathetic agreement. 'But there are some good voices in the company proper,' he said. 'Really astonishing for a new company like this one. It must have been very stimulating to work with them.'

'Yes, yes, very stimulating indeed,' murmured Mr Pettifer. 'Mr Turner has a very good ear for voices, and—' he blinked modestly—'I've suggested one or two names. But the credit is his. He rarely makes a mistake, at least not in voices.'

'You think he makes other sorts of mistake?'

There was a moment of hesitancy. 'Perhaps Mr Caulfield, as it turned out, was not the best choice as resident producer,' Mr Pettifer hazarded timidly. 'But still, opera producers are rare birds, a very small field indeed.'

'And you don't think Miss Ffrench was a mistake?'

'No, no, not at all, not as far as the voice was concerned. He just heard her on stage, you see. You can't pick a company on their personalities—what very odd results you would get.' Mr Pettifer gave a wheezy laugh. 'And it was a good rich voice—very penetrating. No artistic judgement, of course, but she'd only been singing a relatively short time, so there was every prospect of her learning, refining the sort of performance she gave, in time. So it seemed. He never met her off stage, you see.'

'If he had, you think he would have realized there was no hope of her improving.'

'Oh certainly. That was easy to see. Quite incapable of learning anything at all. I fear she would have been in for disappointments, poor girl, if she'd lived. I expect she would have finished up as one of the stars in one of the tiny German companies. They like things overdone in Germany, you know.'

Mr Pettifer's sharp little eyes twinkled. He seemed surprisingly confident in his summings-up of the inadequacies of the great nations of Europe.

'But in fact,' said Nichols, 'as it turned out, Miss Ffrench's engagement was a mistake?'

'Oh yes,' said Mr Pettifer. 'But Mr Turner would have got rid of her as soon as practical: she wasn't contracted beyond Christmas, which was very sensible of him. And Mr Caulfield too: he'd had his doubts about him already, and there were rumours that he didn't get along with Simon Mulley. If we can keep Mulley, we'll be a company to reckon with, I believe.' His eyes twinkled again. 'Perhaps we might even get an adequate grant from the gentlemen in London. So they would both have gone, I'm quite sure. One has to be ruthless in a position like his. Mr Turner knows how to get rid of people.'

Mr Pettifer said this in a matter-of-fact way, as if quite unconscious of its ambiguity.

'You must have had a lot of unpleasantness during the early rehearsals,' said Nichols.

Mr Pettifer shrugged. 'A fair bit, a fair bit.'

'My problem is,' said Nichols, 'that while there seems to have been quite a lot of people who disliked Gaylene Ffrench and thought her a general menace, what I really need to find is someone with a quite specific motive for murdering her.'

'Do you think so?' said Mr Pettifer.

Nichols caught the implied disagreement. 'You think this sort of general dislike was good enough ground, do you?' he asked sceptically. 'You could be right. But she must have packed a real punch when it came to being objectionable.'

'A fairly hefty one, yes,' agreed Mr Pettifer. 'But of course one knows the type. One has met it so often. Simply eaten up with egotism. Nothing exists outside themselves, their immediate satisfactions, their career prospects. They're complete poison, wherever they go. But one does get used to that sort of type, in the theatre. And though she was a pretty good specimen, and would have had to go, still—' the moustache bristled as in his mind he reviewed the theatrical Chamber of Horrors his memory could conjure up—'still, there've been worse. And we all develop some form of protective covering.'

Nichols frowned. 'I thought from what you said that you thought the company's dislike of her was sufficient motive?'

'Oh no, no. I've known people like that in company after company. After a time they become a sort of joke. They're so predictable. You almost get pleasure out of forecasting what they'll do or say. Oh no, they're not the type who get murdered, as a rule.'

Nichols felt irritated, as always when people seemed to be contradicting themselves.

'But the fact remains, whatever view we take of those first two rather feeble attempts, the fact remains that someone went to the lengths of rigging up an elaborate device of wires and doorknobs and metal doormats, simply in order to kill Gaylene Ffrench.'

At that moment the music was swelling out, and from the stage Simon Mulley and Giulia Contini started bellowing to the farthest corners of the theatre about vengeance and forgiveness. In the exciting swell of the music Mr Pettifer's reply got lost. It was not until the duet had drawn to a thunderous close that Nichols turned to him again.

'I'm sorry, I missed that,' he said.

'I said: "or in order to kill Sergeant Harrison",' said Mr Pettifer.

# CHAPTER XVII

*Un Colpo di Canone*

'The fact of the matter is,' said Nichols, sinking into the desk chair of Sergeant Harrison's little office, 'that we've been fools, damned fools, complete and utter idiots.' He thought it best not to involve Sergeant Chappell in his own sins of omission, so he added: 'Or I have.'

'But you can't be sure he's right, can you?' said Sergeant Chappell. 'After all, it's no more than a guess.'

'It's a guess that has a ring of truth, to me at any rate,' said Nichols. 'Think it over: if the murderer was told by Sergeant Harrison that he felt ill and was unlikely to be there next day, or if he heard of it indirectly, then the most likely victim would be Gaylene Ffrench, and we've been along the right lines all along. But if he didn't—and everyone we've spoken to has agreed he was no great talker—then it's practically certain that it would be Harrison himself who would have got his packet, a few hours earlier than he actually did. When he was on duty he did a round of inspection of the dressing-rooms, and everyone in the company would have known that. And we were told it, and we absolutely ignored it.'

'Yes, I can see we shouldn't have done that,' said Chappell.

'And if it had happened as planned, what would we have thought when we came to investigate?'

'That it was the third in the series of attempts on Gaylene Ffrench, and that it had misfired like the earlier ones.'

'Exactly. Fools that we are. But in fact what misfired was the plan, due to Harrison's malaria. At least, that's the assumption I'm going to work on from now on. After all, we have two alternative scenarios. We've investigated the Gaylene angle till we're blue in the face, and we've come up with nothing more concrete than that she was a poisonous piece of goods. It's time to try the second angle, which so far we haven't given five seconds to—that the thing was aimed at Sergeant Harrison.'

'But Harrison was liked—within reason anyway— and we've no more solid motive for killing him than for Gaylene.'

'Because we haven't been looking,' Nichols pointed out. 'He was liked, that's true, but he was also in the sort of position where he might well find out something he was not supposed to find out, and he had the sort of mind that liked to have everything ship-shape and properly ticketed, to know what was going on and why it was going on.'

'And that was why he was killed?' asked Sergeant Chappell sceptically.

'Maybe, maybe,' said Nichols. He paused for a moment, deep in thought. 'I'm trying to think: that first night, when he rang us. What exactly did he say? "I've just remembered something"? No, that wasn't it. "I've only just realized"—that was it. Then he said something like: "I could kick myself for not thinking of it earlier".'

'But what did he mean,' asked Sergeant Chappell, 'if he didn't mean that he'd thought of something, or remembered something—some clue to Gaylene Ffrench's murder?'

'He meant: "I've just realized that it was me the thing was aimed at." I wouldn't mind betting that he also meant: "and I've got a pretty good idea why".'

'And that's what he never lived to tell us,' said Chappell.

'Exactly. That's what we've got to find out.'

The two sat in silence, and both of them were remembering some of the things that Mr Pettifer had said to them, after he had made his stunningly simple suggestion.

'He was a man who had to know things,' he said, with a sort of certainty about other people's characters which comes of years of keeping quiet and watching. 'There wasn't anything underhand or unpleasant about it: he was a very simple man—rigid, rather stupid, perhaps, but straight. But he had an orderly sort of mind, military I would imagine, wouldn't you? And he was surrounded by the usual chaos of the theatre which is perhaps something more than you can really imagine, if you haven't known it—physical chaos, emotional chaos. And he was trying to impose his own sort of order on to it, to find out exactly what people were doing, precisely what their motives were, or what their emotional state was. It wasn't pure prying, but he needed total control over the things around him, if I might put it that way.'

There had been a long pause, during which Mr
Pettifer's little moustache had twitched incessantly.
Then he had said: 'That sort of person is more
likely to get murdered, don't you think, than someone who makes themselves more obviously objectionable? And though theatrical people like to live
on the surface, flaunt their private lives—even make
a pageant of them, like poor Gaylene—still, we all
have our little secrets, our other lives which we
don't want people to pry into, don't we?'

The mind boggled at the thought of Mr Pettifer
having a Mr Hyde side to his character which he
needed to keep hidden from the likes of Sergeant
Harrison, but Nichols had taken his point. In fact
the more he thought over his words, the more completely did they make sense.

When he had mulled over Mr Pettifer's words
yet again, Nichols turned to Sergeant Chappell and
said: 'Well, one thing I'm sure about is that we're
right to keep on with the theatre and the people
in it. That has always seemed most obvious. It has
to be someone who knew which was Gaylene's
dressing-room, and knew about the attacks on
her—the supposed attacks, I should say. I don't
think we need go sniffing around Harrison's private
life—not yet anyway.'

'At least that means we haven't been slogging
away entirely in vain,' said Sergeant Chappell.

'And that being so,' continued Nichols, trying
to put his thought processes into an orderly progression, 'one person stands out as the obvious
candidate, though one could easily make a mistake
there. And even if I'm right, there's no shadow of

a motive, so far as I can see . . .' He thought for a bit. 'I wonder if it's worth . . .'

He picked up the phone, got on to Headquarters, and rapped out a series of questions for an early reply. When he put down the phone he saw a pair of questioning eyes on him.

'Of course, it's only a vague possibility,' he said, 'one of many. All I'm trying to do at the moment is to get my thoughts in some kind of order, now that the case seems to have turned itself upside down. Now, even if we take it that Pettifer is right, there's still one thing that doesn't fit, and bothers me.'

'Something connected with the earlier attacks?'

'No—as I see it, everything fits completely into place there. They must have been the work of Gaylene herself. The girl was ravenous for publicity, she was very stupid, and hardly bothered to make the second one convincing. Anyone else would surely have had the sense to make the gesture of calling the police, but not her. No, all this seems to me to fit completely into place, and granted what we know of the girl it's by far the best and most convincing explanation there is. Remember that she was an athlete, as well as an actress of sorts, so there wouldn't be any problem in falling downstairs without getting badly hurt. No, what worries me is the electrocution attempt.'

'The attempt that worked? Why?' asked Sergeant Chappell.

'Precisely because it seems to me that it couldn't be *relied on* to work. If one was going to take advantage of the attempts on Gaylene to kill Sergeant Harrison, surely one would choose a completely fool-proof method. But this was far from a sure-fire thing—nothing like a gun to the head or a knife in the ribs—what he eventually got, poor bugger. Quite simply, it's a damned dicey way of doing anyone in. Why on earth adopt that method when in your next attempt you're willing to stick a knife into him?'

'Well,' said Sergeant Chappell, 'it seems to tie in with the others—rather jokey, "theatrical" I suppose you might call them. A bit far-fetched and not certain to succeed.'

'Exactly. And I suppose that must be the reason that method was chosen—to fit in with the others. But I'm just wondering if there might be an outside chance that it *was* immaterial to the murderer whether Harrison actually died or not.'

'What do you mean, sir?' asked Chappell, perplexed. 'Surely in view of the actual knifing . . . ?'

'But that was *after* someone had been killed. You might as well get life imprisonment for a sheep as for a goat. And in fact the point might be that once Gaylene had been killed the murderer might have known that Sergeant Harrison would be bound to have suspicions that could lead us to the murderer, so he had to be killed, not incapacitated. But earlier—couldn't it be that the jokey method was adopted partly because it fitted the pattern, but also because the important thing was that Harrison had to be out of the way for a bit, and it didn't greatly matter whether he died or was pretty severely shocked, in both senses of the word. In other words—it wasn't something he knew or suspected, but something he *had*, or something that could only be done with him away. Do you think that could be a remote possibility? Does it make any sense?'

'Yes,' said Sergeant Chappell, trying not to let his dubiousness get into his voice. 'It makes sense if you can think of a reason why.'

'Yes, that's the point,' said Nichols. 'Now, I'm just meditating aloud, but let's try and think this thing through. Now, what would be the major consequences of Sergeant Harrison being put out of action for a bit?'

'Well, said Sergeant Chappell, furrowing his brow, 'I don't think it would make all that much difference. I suppose Bob would take over as stage-door-keeper.'

'Yes—and what would the consequences of that be?'

'Everything run on a looser rein, as far as we've heard.'

'Yes. In other words, there must have been some things that could be done with Bob in charge which couldn't have been done with Harrison poking his sergeant-major's nose into everything.'

The phone rang, and Nichols was on to it in a trice.

'Yes . . . fast working . . . You've nothing concrete on them . . . so it's no more than suspicion really . . . no . . . I *see*, and where does she live? . . . Well, I want her followed—just as soon as you can get on to it . . . Right . . . Keep me posted about that, won't you, and about anything else you dig up . . . Thanks, and keep at it.'

He put down the phone, and as he did so his absorption in the information he had just been given caused him to blink his eyes as he reawoke to his surroundings, as if he wondered where he was. But as he looked around, and came back to the real world, an expression of dubious enlightenment spread over his face.

'I'll tell you what,' he said, turning to Sergeant Chappell, 'one thing you could do with Harrison out of the way that you couldn't do otherwise would be to get in here.'

The woman walked off the boat, casual but business-like, and made her way through the dock area towards the waiting bus. She was a well-preserved forty, and handsome in a hard, determined, nice-as-pie-until-you-cross-me sort of way. She carried herself and her suitcase as if she was used to travelling independently, and she hardly glanced at her fellow-passengers or at the uniformed police dotted around the dock area. Nor did she give any sign of having noticed the two men in the nondescript fawn and white shirts, the casual trousers and the yesterday's hair-styles who detached themselves from the newspaper kiosk and followed her out into the sunlight. Nor did she notice, when she got on the bus to the station, that they stood downstairs some feet away from her, though they very easily could have gone and sat upstairs. In fact, she gave the impression of having something else to think about, for though she sat looking ahead, apparently calmly, she occasionally allowed the suspicion of a frown to furrow her smooth South Sea Island mask of a face. Her oblivion to most of what was going on around her lasted through the transition from bus to train, and through the train journey to Manchester, though the two men with the nondescript shirts were in the next compartment to her, and one or other frequently went out into the corridor to smoke, or to gaze out at the dreary townscape, which would seem to the outsider to offer naught for anybody's comfort.

At her journey's end, she took her suitcase down from the rack, and unhurriedly waited her turn to get into the corridor and out on to the platform. She similarly seemed in no hurry for her taxi, indulged in none of the usual dodges of the impatient traveller, and stood patiently in the queue. She did not appear to notice that the men from the bus and the train, far from waiting in the queue, had placed themselves some way away, though through the co-operation of a waiting constable they secured a taxi just before her, told it to wait a few moments, and then rolled out of the station immediately behind her.

There were too many taxis around the station for the woman to get the idea that she was being followed. Her journey was only a ten-minute one, and when she pulled up outside a decayed and unattractive late-nineteenth-century house of few pretensions she paid no heed to the other taxi which coasted by the end of the street and let its passengers off around the corner. She got out, paid the driver, took her suitcase in her hands, and with barely a glance at the house of her destination, proceeded up the front steps. So that by the time the casual trousers and last-year's haircuts came round the corner, she was already closing the front door and proceeding down the hallway.

By that time, too, a message was going through to police headquarters from the central taxi switch-

board, and a police operation of some magnitude
was being set in motion.

Sergeant Chappell was still dubious, but it didn't
do to express his dubiety too obviously. Rank still
meant something in the force, and experience told
him that it was no better to be sceptical and right
than to be sceptical and wrong.

'It's a thought,' he said, as Nichols, having had
his thought, looked pensively around the room. He
had always found that a particularly useful phrase.

'No more than that,' said Nichols honestly. 'But
it would explain why the electrocution attempt was
such a hit-or-miss sort of set-up. Whether the man
died, or whether he was just badly shocked, the
murderer could rely on his being away for the next
few days, so that this room would be more open
and accessible.'

'Except that we moved in.'

'Exactly. Pure chance—no credit to us for that.
What thundering asses we'll feel if we've been sitting a few feet away from the solution all this time.

'But does that mean, do you think, that he hasn't
been able to do whatever he wanted to do?' asked
Chappell.

'It's a distinct possibility,' said Nichols, 'granted
that I'm on the right lines. Of course there's the
time between the murder discovery and our arrival
—there's the whole of the morning, in fact. But
would he have done it then? Putting myself in his
place, I'm pretty sure I'd have aimed to be away
from the theatre at the time it was likely to happen, and to take advantage of it later. Psychologically that seems the most likely thing.'

'So, if you're right,' said Chappell, 'he must be on the rack, and just itching for us to get out.'

'Yes—unless the removal of Harrison removes much of the danger. The point is—what was the big attraction of a free run of this room? Was he looking for something?'

'Mail, for example?'

'Could be. Someone else's mail it would have to be, presumably. That seems a bit over-complex, though. How would he know what was about to arrive? What about a key? Harrison would be sure to be a stickler about something like that if he was stuffy about mail and lost property. So the only chance of getting hold of one, if you needed it, would be to get him out of the way.'

'A key to some other part of the theatre, you mean?'

'Yes. What could it be—a cupboard, a store-room? Nothing springs to mind that would make it worthwhile to risk a murder rap. Money seems the obvious thing. There wouldn't be any around here, but there could be a key to the box-office safe, or wherever they keep it.'

'But surely even this Bob character wouldn't leave a key like that lying around here for anyone to pick up?' interposed Sergeant Chappell.

'No, you're right. He'd either keep it with him twenty-four hours of the day, or he'd keep it very well hidden. The thought of Sergeant Harrison's wrath would make sure of that. Still, money seems to be the most likely of the things we've considered so far.'

'I suppose Harrison would have had a lot of papers of one sort or another around here, wouldn't he?' said Chappell vaguely. 'You don't think they could tell us anything?'

Nichols rummaged around in the desk he was sitting at, and came up with a handful. He riffled through them sceptically.

'Schedules of various kinds. Rehearsal times and places—for chorus, orchestra, principals. Details of the Pitford Methodist Hall rehearsals and who would be there. Details of who would have which dressing-room on which night. Here's Gaylene down for number five for the seventh—that's right. That room seems to have been kept for the principal mezzo: the girl playing Dorabelle had had it the night before, when *Così Fan Tutte* was being performed. It's all done in a very orderly and ship-shape fashion, Sergeant Harrison was all of a piece —he hangs together, so to speak.'

'More than the rest of this lot do,' said Sergeant Chappell. 'You can see old Pettifer's point about needing to have a bit of order in the midst of chaos. It would drive you mad otherwise. Look at the way he's stored up that lost property, for example.'

Superintendent Nichols allowed his eyes to stray in the direction of the racks at the far end of the room. At one end of the top shelf was a pile of scarves, and next to it a pile of gloves, and next to that a pile of hats three deep, divided into male and female hats, with a few hats of undeterminate sex in the middle. On the next shelf were handbags, shoulder-bags, shopping bags and briefcases. Below that books, newspapers and assorted odds and ends which it needed an imagination of some vivacity to fathom why on earth they should be

taken into a theatre at all. By the side of the racks
was a neat stack of umbrellas.

'The military mind at work,' murmured Nichols.
'You don't think it could conceivably . . .'

'Wouldn't those things have been left by members of the general public?' asked Chappell.

'Not necessarily. I imagine anything left in any
part of the theatre would find its way here.'

'If it was lost by a member of the cast, why
didn't they just come in and ask him for it?'

'That,' said Nichols, getting up, 'is the question.
If there is something among that junk that somebody couldn't well come in and ask for, then we
might have found the answer to the whole question—the reason for the electrocution. Or do you
think I'm completely up the wall?'

'No, of course not,' protested Sergeant Chappell,
as in duty bound. 'But it's only a hunch, isn't it?'

'Less than that, less. But this pile of rubbish
seems the only thing left in the room we haven't
been through yet, and, apart from the keys, it
seems as likely as anything.'

Nichols stopped by the rack and surveyed it.
Ignoring the hats and scarves, he fixed his eye on
the middle shelf, where the bags and cases were.
Over most of them the dust was thick: it was a long
time since people had been able to take such things
into a theatre. Nichols took out gingerly a bulky
shopping-bag, and Chappell followed suit. Together they began working along the row. Methodically they checked through the extraordinary
collection of things people in an affluent society are
apparently willing to leave in a theatre and not
bother to reclaim: library books, perishable foods;

gramophone records; clothes still gift-wrapped from the shop; old sweaters doffed because of the heat; small bogus antiques of one sort or another; the army lists for 1876; a signed photograph of David Frost.

Slowly they worked their way through, Nichols's less-than-hunch seemed frailer and frailer with every bag. Finally Nichols took down the last of the line of briefcases, saying: 'We'd better go back to the handbags, I suppose, just to say we've done the job properly.'

He opened the large briefcase. It was less dusty that the rest. Inside was nothing but a music-score. He was just shutting it when he paused, and slowly raised the bag to his nose. He took a long sniff.

'Good God,' he said to Chappell, handing him the bag. 'Here, take this away from all this musty stuff and get a whiff. Do you smell what I smell?'

Chappell sniffed. 'Christ,' he said. 'I think you're right.'

'Do you remember what I said when we first walked into this room?' asked Nichols. ' "It smells military," I said.'

'Didn't it bloody ever,' said Chappell. 'It smelt of explosives.'

# CHAPTER XVIII

## *First Night*

The Northern Opera Company had had several first nights, both in Liverpool and Manchester, during their first year, but they had had none to match the first night of their second season. It was not quite glamorous, but it was definitely smart. There were several possible reasons for this. The opinion had been gaining ground, fostered by a series of articles and interviews in papers like the *Guardian*, that Mike Turner's plaything was not just a worthy enterprise, but a fine company in the making. This impression had been strengthened by the accession to the company this season of a singer of Simon Mulley's stature, and by the brilliant debut of Bridget Lander. Then again, Mike Turner had had the bright idea of upping considerably the prices of seats for the *Rigoletto* first night—always a bait for the foolish. The murder had naturally done much more good than harm, and it was a fair bet that a delicious frisson would go through the house every time Sparafucile fingered his blade. And last but far from least, Royalty was staying with friends in Lancashire, and the rumour had somehow got around that it would be attending. This proved an irresistible incitement to glitter and dressiness.

So, for one reason and another, the beauty and
fashion of the Manchester district gathered for the
premiere: plump matrons in their fifties, with bare,
freckled arms and long satin dresses edged with
spangly braid; heavy gentlemen, veterans of innu-
merable business lunches, their stomachs conducting a perpetual border warfare with the waistbands
of their trousers, their complexions fiery, their eyes
dulled; hard middle-aged women who were nearly
there but not quite, dragging with them to assert
their claims to social eminence husbands who
looked as if they were tiring of the struggle; and
then the younger set—minor gentry with southern
accents and manners learnt God knows where. All
were there to see and be seen, to sneer and be
sneered at.

In the foyer and bars in the half-hour before cur-
tain-up, they exchanged heavy jokes about the art
of opera which had been elderly in Melba's prime,
they looked at what their husband's partner's wife
was wearing, and priced it; they kept a weather eye
open and a loyal smile at the ready, in case of
Royalty; and they talked about the murders, re-
tailed true and erroneous press stories, passed on
gossip which they claimed to be from their domes-
tics and employees, who had relations working at
the theatre, discoursed with great technical exper-
tise on electrocution as a method of murder, and
indulged in delicious speculation about what their
reaction would be if murder were to be done on
stage that very night.

'I should just faint clean away,' said a woman
who would have watched the St Bartholomew
massacres with polite interest.

Eventually they drifted in, in ones and twos and gossiping groups. The old theatre seemed to cast off a few degrees of dinginess: the dull scarlet of the seats and walls seemed to brighten up by a shade or two, and the gilded cherubs looked golder and younger, as if they were assuring themselves that the good old days were come again. The audience settled in their seats, ate a few chocolates, and read the synopsis in their programmes with sinking hearts. By the time the lights dimmed the whole theatre was full, with the exception of one aisle seat in the tenth row. The rumour went around that this was reserved for Royalty, and this rumour was followed by a pooh-pooh which said that of course Royalty wouldn't come along. Finally it was said that Royalty had in fact already arrived and had gone to the dress circle, and all the stalls craned their necks to try and spot it there. And then the lights went down altogether.

Backstage there was tension, a nervous eyeing of others and a good deal of tittering and backbiting, but the topics of conversation were different from those in the audience. Murder was not mentioned. In fact, if it had been, almost every member of the cast would have started in surprise, and would have had to make a giant effort of memory to gather what was being talked about. Gaylene and Sergeant Harrison were of the past. Owen—whom the press, with fair accuracy, had reported to be suffering from 'nervous exhaustion'—was of the past. The present was a matter of wigs and costumes, the look of a sword, the security of a moustache. The present was a matter of either *the* performance or *their* performance, and every mind was concentrated on one or the other or both. Only rarely could their attention be drawn to anything outside those narrow limits.

'Mike looks worried,' said Calvin to Bridget, as they watched him hurry past like the white rabbit.

'Well, don't pretend you're a stranger to butter-flies,' said Bridget.

'Oh, I'm a wreck. But he's usually as cool as lime-juice. What's this about his wife wanting a divorce—have you heard?'

'Something. What difference would it make? They're never together anyway. Look, when we have the little dialogue after the minuet, could you take my *left* hand, and then turn round, so that we both have our *profiles* to the audience . . .'

The pair were watched greedily by the unemployed school-leaver who had first summoned Bridget to stardom, and who by now was head-over-heels in love with her, with opera, with the theatre and life, and was meditating various fantastic ways of removing Calvin from this world, involving cunningly poised meat-axes, poisoned darts shot at him from the prompter's box, and genuine knives substituted for stage ones. He had become all too well assimilated into his milieu.

Mike Turner did look worried. He looked less than usual like the sort of young man wished on marginal seats by Conservative Central Office. In fact, he gave the impression that in a few years he might well be cultivating that haggard-distin-guished look so popular among musicians. As he walked among the stage-hands and cast he was thinking: All this—just going up in smoke because

that rich bitch has got herself a fancy man with a
title. Just when all the spade-work was beginning
to pay dividends. What chance of coming to an
agreement: a quicky, easy divorce in exchange for
a large cash sum? That at least would keep us
going to the end of the season. Trouble is, she's got
me over a slow fire, so why should she come to an
agreement? There's plenty of big-wigs out there.
No one can say I haven't licked the municipal arse
when necessary. And what have I got out of it?
The chances of a thumping grant from that lot are
precisely nil. In the end, it all comes back to the
Arts Council. We can only carry on if they come up
with a subsidy. And to do that we have to 'prove
ourselves artistically', whatever the stingy bastards
mean by that. What chance of them stumping up?
What chance?

As he arrived behind the orchestra pit and stood
waiting for the lights to dim, two tears forced
themselves to the corners of his eyes. He was thinking of the subsidy paid to Covent Garden.

In the wings everything was poised for the lights
to go down. Simon Mulley was alone, thinking
himself into his part. Everything he could do to improve Owen's conventional-style production had
been done. Now everyone would have to take care
of themselves, even Barbara. Now he had to think
of his own performance. Raymond Ricci, not on
till the second scene, was also apparently thinking
of his own performance. He was prowling around
the wings, a saturnine, threatening presence, now
and then letting his hand stray to the long knife by
his side, and occasionally throwing threatening
glances—or so they seemed, with his sinister make-

up—in the direction of a dark corner, where Giulia
Contini was gesticulating charmingly in conversation with Hurtle Marwick, who had somehow
managed to get backstage. Perhaps he was going
to help shift the scenery. Barbara Bootle was as
usual hugging the darkness, sitting in a corner,
sometimes uttering little groans to herself, but
sometimes looking out at the bustle and seeming to
be affected for the better by the tension and fuss.

Calvin and Bridget stood poised, ready to start
the opera, Calvin wondering how any composer
could expect his tenor to throw off an airy piece
like 'Questa o quella' after less than a minute on
stage, Bridget how one was to make any sort of
impression on an audience in a part that consisted
of two or three phrases. Both were together, in
love, and yet solitary.

And then the lights were finally extinguished,
and Mike Turner made his way through the brass
and strings to take his place on the podium.

The opening chords of the opera, sinister and
threatening, penetrated to the stage-door-keeper's
office as if through a heavy blanket, and Nichols
pricked up his ears.

'Well, they've got started,' he said. 'I hope they're
going to be able to finish.'

'What shall we do if the call comes through during the performance?' asked Chappell.

'We'll have to go in for the kill. We've no option.
We can't police the entire theatre, and anyone
could get a warning in to him. We can't be oh-so-
polite and let them finish if there's any risk of him
getting away.'

'What's Special Branch come up with so far?'

'A lot of interesting stuff, though most of it's not solid as yet. That will depend on the woman. But as far as I can gather they've got the general picture pretty well sorted out.'

'It's not one of the terrorist groups, of course?'

'Oh no—nothing of the kind. I didn't expect that for a moment, not with that sort of chap. It's one of these protection rackets. These last few years they've been like limpets, clinging on to the main part of the Northern Irish problem. They sprang up in Belfast in the early seventies, and they've spread over here in the last couple of years or so.'

'I'd heard of some sort of Catholic outfit operating in Liverpool, but I don't know much about it.'

'Well, both lots have them, and they milk both sides. Religion is pretty irrelevant, of course, with people like that, but officially they retain their allegiances. They get smallish sums out of the Irish businessmen over here—publicans, bookmakers, small shopkeepers, people like that. It becomes a sort of retainer: pay up, and you're safe from both sides.'

'I suppose it's worth their while to pay, when you consider some of the things that have happened over the past years.'

'Yes, I gather the Catholic thugs have made a pretty good thing out of it among the Irish community in Liverpool for a fair while now. The Prots moved in there last year, and now they're extending operations to Manchester.'

'You say it's not a question of enormous sums?'

'Oh no. Just a tidy living for a few crooks and their hangers on. There's been no need for any great degree of violence—just a few "exemplary sentences", as they charmingly call them. A couple of shootings in the knee, three or four minor explosions—enough to put the business out of operation for a week or so. It makes an impression.'

'I'd heard about them of course,' said Chappell, 'but I'd assumed they were just regular IRA feuds. I've never got to the bottom of what goes on among that lot.'

'Has anyone?' said Nichols gloomily.

'So probably there hasn't been any need for huge amounts of explosives or weapons?'

'Oh, I don't imagine the amount of stuff brought in has been all that large. That's why they've got away with it so easily. Mind you, it had all been adding up. They had a fair supply of guns and gelignite at their base—they were planning to extend their operation, that's obvious. Through the North and down to London, I'd guess. Ultimately the tie-up is back to Belfast, and pinning anything on anyone will be one hell of a headache for Special Branch. You know how those tribes cling together.'

'Thank God it's not our responsibility. So we've only come up with one of the small fry? McKaid and his lovely lady wife weren't among the big-boys in the set-up?'

'Oh no—cogs in the wheel. But useful, none the less, because he went between Manchester and Liverpool regularly with the company, and fairly often home to Belfast. She came over every month or six weeks "to be with him", so there was no earthly reason why their comings and goings should rouse comment. She was supposed to be in the audience tonight, by the way. There was always a good excuse for coming over. For them it was a nice little supplementary income, or perhaps a bit better than that. From the look of his flat and his wardrobe I'd guess he had a taste for luxury.'

'Rather tarty, I'd call it,' said Chappell disdainfully.

'He's a back-street boy, not slum but the next worst thing. It often takes them that way. She looked as if she needed to put up a pretty good front to the world as well—underneath the make-up I'd guess she was a hard, bitter sort of person.'

'So at last we have our motive, and it's nothing more than good old-fashioned greed?'

'Exactly—with a small admixture of fear, perhaps. I'd guess that McKaid had very little to do with the gang himself. There were several people involved, and the aim must have been to keep the lower thugs in ignorance of the names and descriptions of the upper thugs. McKaid seems to have been a middle-man—he and his wife—and that's what will make them particularly useful. They brought explosives from Northern Ireland, and they distributed them to the little men when a job was in the offing. Just a simple matter of arranging time and place—often at or near the stage door, I'd guess. Very small-scale—just a couple of guns here, a few sticks of gelignite there.'

'But still worth killing for.'

'Yes, especially in view of the sort of sentence handed out in cases of this kind recently.'

'I suppose something must have gone wrong with the transfer system,' said Chappell.

'Not necessarily. The briefcase was empty—

though there were certainly traces of what it had been used for. I guess he just left it around somewhere backstage by accident, or while he was rehearsing, and Harrison collared it. Everyone in theatres is jumpy about bags and cases these days, probably Harrison more than most. He found it was empty, put it with his collection—but he wasn't happy, and McKaid must have realized he wouldn't be.'

'And the silly chap didn't do anything about it.'

'No—more's the pity for him. Of course, to be fair, all he had to go on was a near-empty briefcase with a smell. Not very much. I expect he just felt vaguely dissatisfied, and stewed it over in his mind. But McKaid would have known he was in a hell of a dangerous position.'

'By then, I suppose, the attacks on Gaylene must have started, mustn't they?' said Chappell.

'Yes, I think so. I'd think he probably rigged up his little device a day or two after he lost the case.'

'Of course, he'd been in on Gaylene's little dodges from the beginning, hadn't he?' said Chappell. 'I suppose the morning after he slept with her she must have got the papers with the engagement of Cross and that Lander girl we never got to talk to, and that gave her the incentive.'

'I'd think it sent her livid with rage—and that's probably why she was by all accounts so horribly convincing when she marched down to the rehearsal and accused them all of it. The gassing wheeze was just the sort of thing to appeal to McKaid's nasty sense of humour, I'd guess, and he probably gave the story a bare minimum of corroboration when necessary. I bet he was glad he did—it came in useful later on.'

'And then when the electrocution failed, he must have had to get Sergeant Harrison as quickly as possible, I suppose,' said Chappell thoughtfully. 'I presume he just went to his house, happened to overhear his telephone conversation with us—'

'It had been a boiling hot day,' put in Nichols.

'Yes—and then waited outside his door and stuck a knife into him. The slum kid's weapon.'

'Quieter than a gun, too, which is a consideration in a built-up area of that kind. Yes, I think as soon as Gaylene was killed instead of Harrison, McKaid must have realized it was a fair bet Harrison would get even more suspicious, and come along to us. And we were bound to connect explosives with Northern Ireland—even two dim-wits as we've proved to be over this case. And then there was *this*.'

He took in his hands the piano score of *Rigoletto* found in the briefcase. He flicked through the pages, all of them clean, until he came to the point in Act II where there were two pencil marks over the part of Marullo so minute that he had to point them out to Sergeant Chappell.

'Harrison can't have seen these, but he was bound to realize their significance if he did decide to look closer. And so would we. No, the two crucial things that decided Harrison's fate were Gaylene being killed and us moving in here. When that happened, Harrison had to be killed.'

The two were silent for a moment. From the stage area still muffled but rather impressive, came the wonderful sound of chorus and powerful voices in full flood.

'How long have they had her now?' asked Chappell at last.

'Special Branch picked her up just after McKaid left his flat for the theatre. She denied all knowledge of the house in Plimsoll Street. She was very cocky and confident, apparently. Not that that kind are necessarily the last to crack. It will depend on how she weighs up the advantages and disadvantages.'

The phone rang, and Nichols was on to it in a flash.

'Nichols here . . . She's cracked—good work . . . Talking nineteen to the dozen . . . No, not yet . . . I see—it could be that she doesn't know much about that . . . Anyway, I'll bring him in and hand him over to you for the moment . . . Be there in a matter of minutes.'

He banged down the phone. 'Right,' he said to Chappell. 'Let's bring him in.'

As they approached the wings, the music swelled out at them with increasing fierceness. Rigoletto had been cursed by Monterone, and Simon Mulley was doing a wonderfully convincing imitation of a superstitious man suddenly caught on the raw—he was cringing and muttering, in so far as one can mutter in a way that reaches more than a thousand people over an orchestra in full flood. He was watched by Calvin, carelessly laughing, by McKaid, sneering, and by the whole line-up of the chorus. As the last chords of the first scene thundered out from the orchestra pit and the great looped curtain swooped down, Nichols and Chappell dived into the shadows at the rear, and watched.

The moment the curtain was down and the applause had begun, the principals began assembling in line for the curtain call, though all around them the noise and chaos of a full-speed change was deafening and bewildering. Mulley, Bridget, Calvin, the singer playing Monterone, and Jim McKaid went to the front of the stage, linked hands, and as the corners of the curtains were lifted went to the front, bowing, curtseying and smirking to acknowledge their reception.

It was James McKaid's last curtain call.

As the curtain came down again, Monterone, the Countess Ceprano and Marullo detached themselves from the line, leaving Calvin and Simon together to take a second curtain. Bridget stood by to hear Calvin's reception, but McKaid plunged through the disorder of scene changers and props towards the wings. At the sight of Nichols and Chappell he pulled himself up: for one second the expression on his face was a question—fight, or flight? But in one second more their hands had come down heavily on his wrists and he was taken into custody, and not even Nichols and Chappell could hear his whines and bluster above the sounds of enthusiasm from the auditorium.

# CHAPTER XIX

*Finale*

Mike Turner saw them taking Jim McKaid away as he came from the back of the orchestra pit to mop his brow during the brief pause between the first and second scenes. One of his many virtues as director of an opera company—one without which no director could retain any remnants of his sanity —was an ability to keep his head. It was based on an inclination to count his blessings.

Thank heavens it wasn't Rigoletto, was his first thought.

His second thought was: what is the done thing in the circumstances? Ought he to cancel the rest of the performance, and go out in front to inform his be-spangled audience that one of his singers had just been hauled off to the jug? No—that was inconceivable. The show must go on—an admirable motto, and one as much to the liking of performers as of audiences, for they seldom feel inclined to let anything prevent them appearing before their public. The cast of *Rigoletto* would be no exception to this rule, and they would be particularly anxious to 'go on' in this case because the only reaction most of them would feel to the arrest of Jim Mc-

Kaid would be a feeling of relief. McKaid had not had the art of pleasing.

Mike Turner strode to the wings.

'They've tekken Mr McKaid,' said the unemployed urchin, who had lived more vividly in the last fortnight than in the entire first sixteen years of his life, and was showing it.

'I know. Where's Pettifer—oh sorry, there you are' (as Mr Pettifer suddenly appeared under his feet). 'We haven't had anyone covering Marullo, have we? Who's the fastest learner among the chorus basses?'

'Well, there's—'

'My brother could do it,' came a voice over Mike Turner's shoulder. He turned. It was, inevitably, the insinuating form of Raymond Ricci, come to assert the continuing strength of the Italian family.

'Could he, do you think? Surely he doesn't know the part?'

'More or less. Marullo's only got two more scenes, and they're both ones with the chorus. He must practically know them already, and he learns very quickly. He'll probably only need to run over the words.'

'Okay. He's on. Where is he—oh' (as the younger, slightly shorter, and not quite so sinister version of Raymond Ricci appeared at his brother's side). 'Get hold of a costume that marks you off from the rest of the chorus. It doesn't matter about the next scene—it's in darkness. Learn your words for the next twenty minutes or so, and then you're on. There's the interval after that: get hold of someone and tell them to make you look as much like McKaid as possible.'

'Nobody notices Marullo,' said Raymond Ricci, 'so it's not that vital.'

'True—which is bloody lucky. Right—I'm going to start Scene II,' said Mike, heading back to the orchestra pit.

It was indeed true that nobody noticed the replacement in the role. In fact, a couple of the London critics mentioned next day that the 'rich young baritone of James McKaid in the role of Marullo', which made them feel fools when they read the news of his arrest on the front pages of the same newspaper. It did seem, though, as if Robert Ricci was fated to get good notices under any name but his own.

Barbara Bootle, leaving her place at the back of the wings whence she had been watching odd fragments of the action through bits of scenery, charged in the direction of the lavatories for the fifth time since the performance started. As usual, by hoping that nobody would notice her, she made sure that everyone did. Her heart was wrung by the look of concern on the face of Calvin Cross.

'You needn't worry,' she said earnestly. 'I'll be all right. I don't mean I'll be all right in the role, but I'll be all right, me.'

'I'm sure you will,' said Calvin.

'I think the arrest has taken my mind off things a bit. And it *is* better not having to wonder whether the person you're singing with is a murderer or not, isn't it? On top of everything else, I mean.'

'It is. And I don't think the performance has suffered, do you? It seems to be going very well.'

'Oh, it *is*. That's what worries me. I'd so *hate* to

let it down.' She headed off miserably in the direction of the loo, and then turned with a pleading expression on her face. 'You will *try* to hide me for as much of the time as possible, won't you?'

In the first interval Mike Turner heard from the front-of-house people that Royalty had indeed come, and was ensconced with friends somewhere in the middle of the dress circle. The news seemed to unnerve him much more than had the arrest of Jim McKaid.

'Good God. Why wasn't I told earlier? What do I do? Go round and welcome them? Is it a large party? Are they in the bar? Couldn't we take them in to one of the private rooms?'

'Since the visit is incognito,' said Bridget calmly, 'I presume the thing that would be most welcome would be to have no notice at all taken of the visit.'

Mike thought for a bit. Then he nodded. 'Yes, that would be best, wouldn't it? We'll pretend we don't know they've come—that's just the thing that never happens to them as a rule. Could someone get on to Publicity and tell them to ring round all the newspapers?'

He looked very pleased with himself at having found The Right Thing To Do in a delicate situation.

The scene between Rigoletto, Marullo and the courtiers had gone very well. Difficulties always spurred Simon Mulley on to give of his best, like most theatrical people, and Robert Ricci as Marullo had done all that was required of him. He had looked a good deal younger than Jim McKaid, but he had sounded considerably fresher.

With the entry of Gilda, after her rape, the tension slackened a little. Simon Mulley was still singing and acting at white heat, but he made little impression on Giulia's placidity. Her solo, and the big duets with Simon, were nice enough to listen to, but they certainly weren't much to watch. Hurtle Marwick, though, was watching her from the wings with considerable admiration. And so was Bridget Lander, with less.

'How's she doing?' asked Calvin.

'Operatic passion—Italian style,' said Bridget, not letting her eyes stray from their intent casing of the stage, her hands clasped tensely together.

'Why are you so interested?' asked Calvin. 'Are you getting the part up for January?'

'I'm noticing what *not* to do,' said Bridget.

'Oh, she's not as bad as all that,' said Calvin, watching.

'She's a second-rate. There's a hundred sopranos in the world who could do the part like that. I'm going to be first-rate.'

Silently Calvin sighed. He was beginning to think it was not going to be the easiest thing in the world—his future as the husband of a great operatic star.

It was the last act that had everyone's hearts in their mouths. Mike Turner had been on hot bricks during the interval: he was torn between the feeling that Bridget's advice about letting Royalty enjoy its evening of pseudo-anonymity in peace

was good sense, and a very strong desire to go and
pay his respects to it, or perhaps invite it back-
stage afterwards. It was not that he expected
CBEs to shower over the company from the royal
hands, nor, indeed, any more tangible largesse.
But still, when you come down to it, Royalty *is*
Royalty.

The tension in Mike was of the sort that had to
find some outlet or other. It communicated itself to
his players, and from the beginning of the last act
a competent, dramatic orchestral performance was
transformed into a blazing one.

Calvin was also tensed up to give of his best.
Like any actor, or any singer with a sense of drama,
there were few moments when he was not acting
in one way or another. The stage was a maggot
that entered the bones very quickly, and when he
was most natural, then he was most subtly acting.
His conversation with Bridget during the closing
duets of Act II had opened his eyes to the new role
that lay ahead for him: the competent tenor husband of the *prima donna assoluta*. The singer who
achieved a tenuous international career by clutching to the skirts of his wife. The singer who received grudging or sneering reviews because the
critics resented the fact that he, rather than Pava-
rotti or Domingo, had been engaged.

During the interval he had squared his shoulders
and said to himself: Some day it will probably be
like that. Some day. But not yet.

By the time he came to sing, the tenseness had
resolved itself into an intoxicating feeling of free-
dom and relaxation. During '*La donna è mobile*' he
discarded the typically Owenish idea of putting

one foot on to the inn bench and holding a goblet aloft, and instead he strolled around the stage, looking at everything with a sort of boyish delight at the unsalubriousness of his surroundings. And when Barbara appeared, hot foot from the loo, but summoning wonderful resources of Lancashire doggedness to carry her through, he threw himself on her, nearly ate her alive to shield her as much as was practicable from the audience's cynical gaze, and as soon as possible got her down on to the bench in a close, sweaty, all-concealing embrace. As he threw himself over her, a thought occurred to him: wouldn't Gaylene be surprised!

And he launched himself, gloriously free and seductive of voice, into the great quartet.

Nichols stood at the door of the stage-door-keeper's room and looked around it for the last time. He had tidied up the mess on the desk, tipped a mountain of alibi cards neatly into envelopes, and rubbed off the dirty black marks his shoes had made on the desk. As he looked along the neat shelves of lost property, the post-racks waiting to be used again, the hooks for keys, with each one labelled, he made a mental bow in the direction of Sergeant Harrison, and hoped he was satisfied.

Tomorrow Bob would move in, and everything would begin to return to normal. But normality would be a looser, more slapdash state than it had been under the redoubtable sergeant. Perhaps it was just as well. Probably a theatre could only stand so much discipline. More than that was dangerous.

And tomorrow he, Nichols, would join with Spe-

cial Branch, and together they would grill McKaid
and his wife and the other members of the repulsive little gang they had managed to pick up—grill
them over and over, till they tired, contradicted
themselves, implicated themselves, betrayed each
other. And after they were done and sizzling, there
would be charges—conspiracy, extortion, maiming,
and against one, murder. It was not a process he
liked being part of. It was his job's equivalent of
lavatory duty.

Meanwhile there was home. Not bad—home before half past ten. There hadn't been many eve-
nings like that in the past week or so. His wife
would be waiting for him, and perhaps they would
have a drink together. Perhaps even a record. Not
*Rigoletto*. Definitely not *Rigoletto*. Perhaps *Ernani*
—always a favourite, whatever the mood. Or perhaps some of the soupier bits of *Rosenkavalier*
would fit the bill.

He turned off the light and shut the door. As his
feet were on the point of directing themselves towards the stage-door, they were caught by the
music, and they turned themselves automatically
towards the stage, where the quartet was swelling
and fading with an irresistible pulse towards its
climax. He walked along the passage as the applause rang out, caught by a spell that had be-
witched him when he was fifteen and had never
lost an iota of its potency. He heard, from his rest-
ing position near the wings, the furtive dialogue
that ensued between Rigoletto and Sparafucile.
Then, unable to stop himself, he opened his mouth,
and in a modest but pleasant baritone he joined in
with Simon Mulley:

'His name is CRIME, and mine is PUNISH-MENT'.

Seeing, from the wings, a row of faces turned on him with scandalized reprobation, he blushed violently, turned on his heels, and made for home.

The cheers rang through the theatre, raucous cheers such as can only be wrung from a jewel-studded, brass-weighted audience by a performance of tremendous passion. Ebullient cheers that brought even the bar-room ladies out to see, and made the gilded cherubs grin with pleasure. It was the most exciting music of the whole evening to the cast lining up to take their curtain-calls. As the curtain was swept aside over and over again, they gazed out on their acclaimers with a modicum of pretended humility, and a great deal of real self-satisfaction. There was not one of them that didn't think in his heart of hearts: We deserve this.

As Barbara Bootle took her solo curtain-call—polite, sympathetic applause, mingled with some patriotic Lancashire encouragement to a native daughter—she was thinking: Perhaps I *won't* ask to go back to the chorus. After all, there *are* some parts I could do properly.

As he took his curtain-call, Raymond Ricci was remembering some words Giulia Contini had hissed at him as he bundled her into her sack: 'You take your dizgusting 'ands off me,' she had said. 'Is finito—understand?' And Raymond was thinking: That bloody little Italian bitch has thrown me over.

As he took his rapturous curtain call, Calvin Cross was thinking: I was good tonight. Damned good. Tonight I'm the star. It can't last, but tonight it's me.

As she took her curtain call—an avalanche of shouting, because this audience would have cheered a steam kettle if it had had an Italian name—Giulia Contini was thinking something very physical about Hurtle.

As he took his curtain call, during which the gallery exploded, Simon Mulley was thinking: This time was good. Perhaps eighty per cent right. Next time, ninety. And after that—

And as Mike Turner took his solo call as conductor he drank in the enthusiasm from every corner of the theatre, blinked into the darkness, and thought that somewhere out there was sitting 'cello-playing, Goon-Show-loving Royalty, and he said to himself: Surely, when Royalty comes along, they're finally going to admit that we've proved ourselves artistically.

And, strange as it may seem, he was probably right.

**SCENE OF THE CRIME**

# ROBERT BARNARD

### Keen on "whodunits" in the classic British style? You'll find these, dear reader, bloody good —and murderously funny.